"It'll be dark soon."

Isabella cast her eyes upward, where the first hints of fiery gold touched the horizon, and set flame to her auburn hair.

"All the more reason to put some miles between us and our new friend," Jacob replied.

She glanced back toward the cavern and the swept-bare sand between them. The black helicopter could return at any moment.

Jacob turned to assess the back exit of the cavern, toward the low, rocky escarpment. He tried to picture the land as he'd seen it in those last few minutes before the crash. His mental map, along with what he remembered from the flight charts, said that if they headed west and slightly north, a stiff three-day hike would bring them to civilization.

And between the crash site and civilization?

He would deal with the hit man as best he could. Capture him if lucky. Kill him if necessary.

Whatever it took to keep Isabella safe.

Jessica Andersen

BULLSEYE

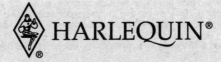

HARLEQUIN®

TORONTO • NEW YORK • LONDON
AMSTERDAM • PARIS • SYDNEY • HAMBURG
STOCKHOLM • ATHENS • TOKYO • MILAN • MADRID
PRAGUE • WARSAW • BUDAPEST • AUCKLAND

Special thanks and acknowledgment are given to
Jessica Andersen for her contribution to the
BIG SKY BOUNTY HUNTERS series.

For Kim Nadelson,
an editor who knows how to make a story sing.

ISBN 0-373-22868-6

BULLSEYE

www.eHarlequin.com

Printed in U.S.A.

ABOUT THE AUTHOR

Though she's tried out professions ranging from cleaning sea lion cages to cloning glaucoma genes, from patent law to training horses, Jessica is happiest when she's combining all these interests with her first love: writing romances. These days she's delighted to be writing full-time on a farm in rural Connecticut that she shares with a small menagerie and a hero named Brian. She hopes you'll visit her at www.JessicaAndersen.com for info on upcoming books, contests and to say "hi"!

Books by Jessica Andersen

Don't miss any of our special offers. Write to us at the following address for information on our newest releases.

Harlequin Reader Service
U.S.: 3010 Walden Ave., P.O. Box 1325, Buffalo, NY 14269
Canadian: P.O. Box 609, Fort Erie, Ont. L2A 5X3

CAST OF CHARACTERS

Jacob (Bullseye) Powell—The sexy ex-Special Forces airstrike pilot is now a Big Sky bounty hunter and a confirmed bachelor. But does an old college flame have the power to change that when she finds herself in danger?

Isabella Gray—The no-nonsense Secret Service agent is all about her duty…until her protectees are abducted and she is forced to turn to the one man she'd hoped never to see again.

Louis Cooper—The U.S. Secretary of Defense will not negotiate with hostage takers. Or will he?

Boone Fowler—The head of the Montana Militia for a Free America has no problem with kidnapping Cooper's family…or killing an interfering Secret Service agent.

Hope Cooper—When she and her twin daughters are abducted, Louis's wife has only survival on her mind.

King Aleksandr of Lunkinburg—The despotic ruler of a small former Soviet bloc country has no apparent ties to Boone Fowler and his men.

Prince Nikolai—Denounced by his father for his patriotic ideals, the prince finds an ally in Louis Cooper, until the Secretary abruptly reverses his position on sending troops into Lunkinburg.

Lyle Nelson—After Isabella shoots him in the leg, Lyle wants revenge—the more painful, the better.

Prologue

Early September in Montana was chill and damp, like fear.

Derek Horton paused at the dark, rocky opening and a shiver crawled down his back. *It's just the drizzle,* he told himself, but it was more than that.

The mouth of the abandoned mine beckoned with the promise of safety, of supplies and a place where the eight fugitives could light a small fire undetected. But the darkness beyond seemed to shift with something else.

A tall man with slashing scars on his face, a scruffy beard and his hair drawn into a warrior's ponytail paused at Derek's side. "Problem?"

Derek shook his head quickly, lest Boone Fowler think him weak or disloyal to The Cause, both of which could be fatal. "No problem. Just taking a quick breather."

"Well, take it inside." The leader of the Montana Militia for a Free America—MMFAFA—jerked his head at the six men strung out in a quiet line behind him. "We need to get out of sight. Those bounty hunter bastards might not be looking in the right places yet, but you can bet they're looking."

Boone's command overrode Derek's dislike of the cavern they had hidden in since their escape from The Fortress—the Montana State Penitentiary. He stepped through the gaping rock maw, into the strange warmth the cave seemed to ooze like sweat.

Rough hands grabbed him the moment he crossed into darkness.

Derek shouted and struck out, but missed. His brain shouted, *Bounty hunters!*

"Get in here, all of you!" a man shouted. "Now!"

His accent was clipped and foreign. Not the bounty hunters, Derek realized as dark-clothed men swarmed around Boone and the others.

Something far worse.

"Let me go!" Panicked, Derek thrashed, then gargled when his captor tightened the arm across his throat, cutting off his breath. His vision grayed, but not before he saw that the others had been similarly subdued.

Boone stood in the center of the small cavern, hands held away from his sides. Two black-clad figures held automatic weapons on him, according him the respect of a leader. Six other ninja types surrounded the remaining MMFAFA members. Derek saw Lyle, Boone's second-in-command and the hothead of the group, spit at one of the gunmen.

The bastard rammed the muzzle of his weapon into Lyle's stomach, sending him to his knees.

Another dark figure stepped into Derek's view, this

one unarmed, though he radiated power and grace. Leadership.

Derek held still, heart pounding. This had to be the man Boone had made a deal with, the man who had helped break them out of The Fortress in exchange for…favors.

"I know what you're thinking," Boone said, staring the cloaked figure in the eye and speaking leader to leader, even though he was being held at gunpoint. "We were unable to complete our first mission. But I have an idea about—"

"Your ideas don't interest me," the black-cloaked man interrupted with a vicious hiss. "I am here to tell you what you will do next. This time it *will* be done correctly, do you understand?"

After a cold, frozen moment, Boone nodded. "I understand. Tell me what you want us to do."

"Not yet. First, I believe a lesson is in order." The figure nodded toward the man behind Derek.

"No. Don't…please don't!" Icy fear splashed in Derek's veins when the dark man's cold gaze fixed on him. He struggled, but to no avail. His captor remained immovable, like the stone surrounding them. Derek reached toward the other militiamen, toward his leader. "Boone, don't let them! Don't!"

But the leader of the MMFAFA said nothing.

The dark figure gestured for Derek's captor to take him deeper into the cavern and said, "You and your men have failed once. That cannot and will not happen again. Understood? If it does, you will face a fate similar to the one your friend is about to meet."

"No-oo!" Derek thrashed madly as he was dragged backward, deeper into the shadows. His heels gouged the soft soil on the cavern floor, sending up a rotten, coppery smell.

"Quiet." Derek's captor tightened the arm across his throat. The lack of oxygen quickly brought dizziness, then the gray of tunnel vision.

Through his narrowed cone of focus, he saw the dark leader step into view, calmly screwing a silencer onto the barrel of a semiautomatic pistol. The man barked a few syllables in a harsh, unfamiliar tongue and tossed Derek against the rock wall with bruising force.

The gunman shrugged and answered in heavily accented English. "I do not wish to bring this whole god-forsaken place down around our ears. I simply wish to teach these idiots a lesson."

With that, he lifted the weapon and fired.

Derek heard the puff of a silenced bullet.

Then nothing.

Chapter One

"Bull!" Jacob Powell grinned and reclaimed his seat near the built-in fridge.

"Big surprise," grumbled fellow bounty hunter Anthony Lombardi. He pulled Jacob's dart from the center of the dartboard and took his place behind the tape mark on the floor. "We don't call you Bullseye for nothing."

The dark-haired hunter threw and hit the inner ring one step out from the center, eliciting howls of derision from the half dozen men gathered in the rec room of the Big Sky Bounty Hunters' headquarters in Ponderosa, Montana.

The rules for Bull were simple. You had five shots. You hit five bullseyes or you lost. And Jacob never lost.

Though he'd earned his nickname in the Special Forces, where he'd been a fighter pilot with an airstrike hit record second to none, the moniker had stuck when he and the rest of the unit had followed their leader, Cameron Murphy, into the bounty hunting business. In his five years as a bounty hunter, as in his Special Forces career, Jacob almost never missed his target.

Failure wasn't an option for Bullseye.

But at that moment, he wasn't thinking about the past, or even about darts. His mind was focused, as it usually was these days, on the job. Though he'd instituted the game of Bull to give his ever-active hands and body something to do, his brain crunched the data he'd assembled on their current bounty.

Too damned little information as far as he was concerned. A few weeks earlier, eight prisoners had done the unthinkable and escaped The Fortress, the nearby maximum-security prison. Big Sky hadn't recaptured them, and worse, the escapees had wreaked havoc, executing a German diplomat and engineering a train crash that had killed the corrupt governor of Montana. The incidents had almost upset months of delicate United Nations' negotiations regarding the despotic king of a former Soviet Bloc country called Lunkinburg.

Almost.

"Your turn, Powell." Tony clapped him on the shoulder. "And Bull."

Meaning that Tony had gotten his five center hits. It was up to Jacob to finish the game with five of his own.

No sweat.

Jacob stood and stepped up to the masking tape line. A television babbled in the background, perpetually tuned to a twenty-four-hour news station. The Secretary of Defense's familiar hangdog, bespectacled face filled the screen as Jacob took aim and buried his first dart in the bullseye.

"Turn up the volume," one of the other bounty hunters ordered. "He's talking about Lunkinburg." Secretary

Cooper, the President's primary adviser on foreign affairs, was strongly in favor of sending troops into the small country.

Jacob sent his second dart whistling into the bull, but focused part of his attention on the secretary's words. The Big Sky Bounty Hunters rarely worked internationally, but the Lunkinburg issue had become their problem the moment their bounty had started targeting diplomats.

Which itself was a puzzle, as Boone Fowler and his followers were strictly domestic hell-raisers. Their agenda was to overthrow the U.S. government in the name of The Cause, which was pretty much defined by Fowler himself and included a dizzying mix of xenophobia and anarchy. This was the first time the MM-FAFA had dabbled in international politics, which begged the central question.

Why now? Why had they broken out of The Fortress and immediately changed their MO?

Secretary Louis Cooper's televised voice said, "The United States military is not the world's police force. However, there is a time and a place for us to say *enough.*" Cooper rested his hands on the wheeled podium in front of him. His faded blond hair was washed out by the lighting, his blue eyes emphasized by the subtle gleam of a navy tie. As Jacob watched, the camera panned out far enough to show brilliant fall colors and a familiar logo.

A quiver of interest ran through him at the sight. The Golf Resort. The Washington, D.C.–based Secretary of Defense was at a Montana vacation spot, not twenty miles away from the log cabin that held the bounty hunters' offices on the main floors and a host of specialized, high-security rooms belowground.

In one of the aboveground rooms, Jacob threw. Bull. Three down, two to go.

Cooper's televised voice continued. "The President, myself and the members of the United Nations have had *enough.* The atrocities perpetrated by King Aleksandr have gone on too long with no hope of change in sight. We must commit to overthrowing Aleksandr's tyrannical rule—a goal that is strengthened by the support we have found within his family."

Jacob focused. Threw. Bull.

On screen, Secretary Cooper gestured toward a midthirties, dark-haired man in a custom-tailored suit. "Please welcome Lunkinburg's premiere freedom fighter. Disowned by his father for his politics, he only wants what is best for his people." Cooper waved the man forward. "I give you Prince Nikolai of Lunkinburg."

Jacob imagined teenage girls swooning all across America at the sight of the crown prince, whose camera appeal was second only to his patriotic fervor.

There was scattered applause from those assembled at the Golf Resort, and the cameras panned to track the prince as he made his way to the portable podium. The image swept over several navy-suited figures in the background. Secret Service most likely, Jacob thought, and ignored the quiver in his gut and the sudden desire to stare at the screen.

He focused instead on the dartboard, where he was one bull away from his usual perfect score. He lifted the missile and felt the click as he visually connected with his target. Measured. Pulled back.

A flicker of navy suit on the screen caught his peripheral view and yanked his attention to the TV in an instant. Images jammed his brain. An hourglass shape. A chin-length swing of auburn hair too vivid to be strawberry-blond, too rich to be brassy red. Flashing green eyes and mobile lips made for kissing.

Jacob's stomach knotted.

He threw.

He missed.

The room stilled with a collective hiss of indrawn breath as the six other bounty hunters stared at the dart quivering in the outer ring of the board. A half an inch farther out and he would have missed the board entirely. In the game of Bull, that entitled the other player to a future claim.

In five years, Jacob had never given up a future claim. Shoot, he'd only missed the bull one other time—and then he'd had a bullet wound in his arm and a temperature well over a hundred and two.

But hell and damn, he'd missed this time. Missed big.

On the television screen, Prince Nikolai spoke of patriotism and human rights, and of how his pain at working against his father was offset by the knowledge that the people of Lunkinburg needed his help. But Jacob heard the words as background noise—his whole attention was locked on the woman standing behind Secretary Cooper with a clever communications device in her ear and an I'm-all-about-the-job look on her face.

His body flashed hot then blazed to nuclear temperatures as he took a second look and realized that, yeah, it was her, all right, a heart-stopping face and mind-blowing body straight out of his past.

Isabella Gray.

HER DAY HAD STARTED well before dawn and didn't look as though it was going to be over anytime soon.

Special Agent Isabella Gray unobtrusively shifted on her aching feet, one level of her consciousness wishing for a shower and a couple of aspirin while another, deeper level scanned the crowd and monitored the low-level chatter on the airwaves. As the single Secret Service agent overseeing the Secretary of Defense's vacation, she'd liaised with the Montana locals for backup and security when Cooper had announced he was holding an impromptu press conference at the resort.

So far, everything seemed under control.

It had better be, she thought with a frown. She'd been up at 3:00 a.m. overseeing the last of the details. It was her event, her security, and her reputation on the line.

They didn't call her a cojone-busting nitpicker for nothing. She didn't tolerate screwups, either above or below her position.

And certainly not from herself.

"And so," Prince Nikolai said into the microphone from his position between two of his personal bodyguard/advisers, "It is with both sadness and joy that I proclaim my support of the UN resolution to send troops into Lunkinburg and remove my father, King Aleksandr, from his dissolute throne." Nikolai glanced at Secretary Cooper. "It is my fondest hope that these actions will bring to my country the great peace and prosperity enjoyed by the people of the U.S., such as Secretary Cooper and his lovely family."

At that, the two men shared a handshake while reporters shouted easily ignored questions.

Secretary Cooper shook his head. "I'm sorry, folks. No questions today. The prince has a prior commitment and I promised to have an early dinner with Hope and the girls."

At the mention of his family, Cooper's normally fierce expression softened so slightly that Isabella might have missed it if she hadn't known to look. But in the past couple of weeks, ever since Cooper had received graphic death threats from King Aleksandr's supporters and been assigned Secret Service protection, she had gotten to know her protectee and his family. For all that he was a political barracuda, Louis Cooper was soft as mush when it came to his young wife, Hope, and his twin, eighteen-month-old daughters, Becky and Tiffany.

Isabella motioned for the locals to flank her, guarding the secretary and Prince Nikolai while they walked from the front of the Golf Resort to the rear, where Cooper's secure chalet was set back against the edge of the dense forest. While she scanned the crowd and the manicured lawns beyond, a small, not-so-easily ignored part of her felt a wistful tug at Cooper's devotion to Hope and the girls.

Isabella had once dreamed of having a loving, stable family of her own, but it hadn't happened. Now, at thirty-five, she protected other people's families and considered it a patriotic trade-off. Even the low-grade maternal urges had mostly faded over the years. She told herself she was only feeling them now because she'd been spending so much time around Becky and Tiff. She told herself it had nothing to do with being in Montana, with knowing that the Big Sky Bounty Hunters were quartered nearby.

But she was lying to herself, and knew it. Damn Jacob Powell. Thirteen years later she still couldn't stop herself from keeping track of him. She'd even located the Big Sky headquarters on a map and checked how long it would take her to reach the cabin.

Not that she'd drop in for a visit. No way, no how. Their relationship had burned comet-bright, and when it had crashed, she'd been left cratered. Nearly destroyed.

She had grown up and grown out of the breakup damn quick, but that didn't mean she'd feel comfortable seeing him again. Besides, what was the point? They were different people now, with different agendas.

He probably barely even remembered her.

And heck, it wasn't as though she thought of him on a weekly basis now, or even yearly. It was being in Montana that had brought him to mind. Montana and the little girls and the foolish dreams she'd once had.

Secretary Cooper and Prince Nikolai stopped on the wide pathway outside the Coopers' chalet, bumping Isabella out of her unproductive, unprofessional thoughts.

"I will leave you here, my friend," Prince Nikolai announced.

The men shook hands and parted, the prince returning up the walkway and passing near Isabella. She caught a faint whiff of his cologne, felt a whisper of his sheer animal magnetism and held herself professionally distant when he stopped a breath away and looked down at her with dark, almost ebony eyes.

"Keep him safe, Agent Gray," the prince said in his trademark low, sexy voice. "I need him. My people need him." He glanced back. "And he is a good man."

"He's my protectee," Isabella said simply, refusing to credit the fine buzz running along her skin, which served only to remind her how long she'd focused on being a Secret Service agent rather than a woman.

The prince held her eyes for a moment more before nodding. "I leave him in your care, then."

She watched him go. Part of her appreciated the aesthetics of his rear view while another wondered why the sexy prince brought nothing more than a pleasant buzz when Jacob—there he was again, darn him—had brought roaring heat that had charred her from the inside out and left her hollow and filled at the same time.

Irritated with her lack of focus, she followed Secretary Cooper into the chalet, scoped out the three-thousand-square-foot vacation palace and checked the perimeter motion detectors to make sure nothing had changed in the hour they'd been gone. As she did her job, she shoved the distractions to the back of her mind.

Nothing seemed out of place. When she returned to the stone-accented great room, King Aleksandr scowled out of the flat screen TV that dominated the opposite wall.

Secretary Cooper cranked up the volume.

"...a traitor to my blood and to my family," the king shouted, red-faced. "The American people should be warned!"

A frisson worked its way through Isabella's gut at the near-threat. The ornate stonework and tapestries visible in the background indicated that Aleksandr was still holed up in his palace in Lunkinburg, but too many incidents in recent years had shown that evil men could cause trouble from afar.

Aleksandr leaned close to the microphone, bringing his flinty gray eyes and heavily lined face into sharp focus. "If Louis Cooper brings war to my country, then his family and the American public will suffer the consequences."

The shiver worked itself into full-blown battle readiness. Isabella locked eyes with Cooper, who warned, "That bastard better not touch Hope and the girls."

"Agreed." She reflexively checked the semiautomatic pistol she carried in a holster at the small of her back. "I'm going to call the Great Falls field office. To hell with them being short staffed, I need backup." She frowned. "I think we should return to Washington. The Service can protect you and your family better there."

God knows her hands were tied out here, with most of the active protection agents either overseeing the President's fund-raising efforts or keeping tabs on the last of the UN diplomats as they left the country.

"Of course." Cooper nodded shortly. "I hate to interrupt our vacation, but my family's safety comes first." He spun on his heel and left the room.

"Yeah," Isabella said into the empty space. "I know." And she shouldn't envy that. She had chosen her path, and though it might not have been the happily-ever-after she'd envisioned in college, the lifestyle fit her like a second skin now, one that she wasn't sure she would want to peel off if offered the chance.

Frankly, she wasn't sure she could.

Cooper returned moments later and gave her a sharp nod. "We'll be ready to go in an hour. Hope is making the necessary arrangements."

"Fine," Isabella said, already forming a mental list of the calls she needed to make. "I'll just—"

Boom! A catastrophic explosion ripped her words away and flung her across the room. She slammed into the wall and lost her breath, her senses. After a moment her vision came back, gray and fuzzy.

Louis Cooper lay flat on the floor, unmoving. Hope reeled from the bedroom, blond hair flying wildly, red-painted mouth open in an *O* of horror, hands out-stretched toward her husband.

Percussion bomb, narrow focus, Isabella's brain supplied, quickly naming the device. The ringing in her ears faded within moments and her arms and legs twitched with returning consciousness. Heart pounding, she dragged herself up and fumbled for the gun at the small of her back. She shouted, "Hope, get back! Get the girls!"

At least she thought she shouted the words. She couldn't hear a thing over the buzzing and the rush of blood through her body.

Three men charged into the room, heavily armed and running low. Their faces were cloaked in rubber Halloween masks of former Presidents Johnson, Clinton and Nixon, which gave the scene a surreal feel.

Nixon and LBJ reached for Secretary Cooper.

"Get away from him!" Isabella yanked up her weapon and fired in one smooth move, but her target jerked aside at the last possible moment. The shot ricocheted off the fieldstone fireplace in the sunken living room and spent itself in a bullhide sofa.

She squeezed off a second round and hit Nixon in the leg. He cursed and went down as she struggled to her feet.

Clinton rushed at her. "Bitch!"

She spun in a dizzy circle and fumbled to bring her weapon up even as the knowledge beat in her veins— *I've got to protect Cooper and his family.*

Her third shot went wild. LBJ closed in from the other side, reversed his weapon and swung it at her head in a deadly arc. She aimed between his eyes and—

Blackness.

IN HIS SMALL OFFICE on the second floor of the Big Sky headquarters, Jacob scrubbed his hands through his short, spiky brown hair, hoping to take away his headache with the gesture. No dice, but maybe he deserved the pain. He'd pretty much pushed himself into the ground since that afternoon, first with a long, hard run through the woods, then with an impromptu sparring session in the gym that Cameron had finally halted due to one too many bloody noses.

Maybe it wasn't pain he was feeling in his head, Jacob thought as he rolled the chair back to the computer and pulled up his e-mail messages, hoping for a lead. Maybe it was anger.

Over the past thirteen years he'd learned to keep his

emotions in check, learned to—mostly—control his temper.

But one sight of Isabella and there it was, front and center in his soul.

Anger. Guilt. Regret. Relief.

He hadn't seen her since the day after they had both graduated from Georgetown. The day he had ended a relationship that had been too intense, too overwhelming for him to stay in and not lose himself.

He cursed and pushed away from the computer and the pitiful amount of information he'd managed to amass in an evening of data mining and phone calls.

Why was he thinking of her at all? How could a single glimpse of her put him back in that roiling, all-consuming place where he barely knew his own name? A place he intended never to go again.

She was nearby. That was why he was thinking of her. It was bad enough he'd glimpsed her on TV and felt the lightning bolt hit his gut. It was worse to learn she'd accompanied the Secretary of Defense on his annual vacation, where Louis Cooper invariably rented the same chalet at the same expensive adult playground.

The Golf Resort. Half an hour away by Jeep, less by horse if he cut up and over the mine-riddled ridge.

Not that he would do any such thing. Why would he? They were nothing to each other now. Ancient history. A bad taste at the back of his mouth.

But damn, she'd looked good on that TV screen. Good enough that several hours, one run and three mock fights later, his body still revved on overdrive from the sight of her, from the memories he'd tried to forget over the years.

Memories of sexual delirium. Sensual oblivion.

The ding of an incoming e-mail message was a relief and Jacob swung back to the keyboard just as voices rose outside the small office. It sounded as though the other bounty hunters were starting a new game of Bull, but he wasn't in the mood anymore. He wanted to work.

He opened a message from Aimelee, a friend at the dispatcher's office. Though he'd flirted briefly with the busty blonde when she'd moved to the area, nothing had come of it. She didn't do the casual thing and he didn't want anything else. So they'd become, surprisingly, friends.

No sighting of the fugitives, her e-mail reported, but a small walk-in clinic was broken into a couple of hours ago. Normally we'd think drugs, but mostly bandages and supplies were taken. Maybe that's something?

Maybe. Jacob typed a quick thanks while his mind poked at the new information.

The fugitives were still in the area—or had been a week earlier when they'd derailed a train carrying a handful of UN diplomats. He bet they were still in the area. Where else would they go? The Montana mountains formed their home base. But where were they hiding? And why the medical supplies?

Perhaps they were nursing wounded from the train sabotage. Or perhaps—

He heard a loud shout outside the office. Running

footsteps. A barked command muffled by the closed door. His heart rate picked up.

What the hell?

He was out of the computer chair and halfway across the office when Tony Lombardi yanked open the door. "Get out here. Now."

Jacob followed his teammate out to the main room. There were only a half dozen bounty hunters in the HQ at that moment, but the knot of men near the front door seemed made up of twice that. He paused at the edge of the crowd. "What's wrong?"

Then he caught a glimpse of auburn hair and a softly rounded cheek. A flash of green eyes. Kissable lips tipped down in a frown of pain, of worry.

The air backed up in his lungs and something hot and mean and messy fisted in his chest. The others moved aside, but he remained paralyzed. "Isabella?"

Even as his brain grappled with her presence, he noted the dusky bruise spreading along her cheek, the unfocused glaze in her eyes. Her clothes were clean, as though she'd taken time to change before finding him. But someone had roughed her up. Hard.

Primal, pure rage roared through him at the sight of an injured woman. At the sight of *this* injured woman. He bit off a curse. "What happened? Who did this?"

Her eyes focused. Flashed. She reached out toward him, then hesitated and glanced at the others. She let her hand drop and said, "Jacob. I need to speak with you. Privately."

Her voice was lower than he remembered. Huskier. Her face and slight body still held hints of the same arcs and sweeps of curve and line. But the edge was new. As was the strength that kept her upright against her injuries.

Aware of his teammates looking on, Jacob reached out and touched a spreading bruise. "Tell me who did this. I'll kill them."

In the moment of silence that followed his declaration, he realized two things. One, he meant every word of it. He'd gladly kill whoever had laid a hand on her. And two, the whip of heat and power that flared up his arm and exploded in his chest warned him that it was still there. The thing that had brought them together over a game of darts in Smiley's Pub in D.C. hadn't died.

God, he wished it had.

He yanked his hand away and scowled. "Names. I want names."

Thirteen years ago she would have told him everything in a rush. He expected the same now, because when you came down to it, people didn't change that much over time.

Instead she narrowed her eyes. "This isn't for public consumption. Can we go someplace more private?" When he didn't budge, she hissed a curse. "Why did I even bother? I knew I shouldn't have come here." She spun and took two steps toward the door.

And collapsed.

"Isabella!" Jacob caught her on the way down. When the others surged forward to help, he swept her up into his arms and tried to brace himself against the feel of her lithe, toned body against his chest. "Stand down, I've got her."

"That's the chick we saw behind the Secretary of Defense," Tony said. "The one who made you miss the Bull."

"No kidding." Jacob carried her to the stairs and started up with no real plan.

"Has something happened to Louis Cooper?" Cameron Murphy asked, his voice carrying the weight of leadership and surprising Jacob, who hadn't even noticed the boss's arrival.

"You'll know as soon as I do." But the thought of it grabbed at Jacob's guts and wouldn't let go. If the Secret Service had been protecting Cooper, it was because he was in danger.

And given that Cooper's protection agent was unconscious half an hour away from the resort—

It didn't look good.

Chapter Two

Isabella couldn't believe she'd fainted. How embarrassing. Worse, she was pretty sure Jacob had seen her hit the floor.

But that was nothing compared to the ultimate shame. She'd failed her protectee. She made a small sound of distress and clamped her eyelids shut against the remembered images.

"I know you're awake." Jacob's low, half-familiar voice seemed to come from far away, making her aware of the yielding surface beneath her and the sense of being in a quiet space amid action. "You said you wanted to talk privately. So talk."

She wanted to tell him to go away and leave her alone. But she had come to him, not the other way around, and she still couldn't talk herself out of the logic.

Within an hour of the attack, she'd found herself kicked out of Cooper's chalet and cut off from all the official options. Refusing to give up on her duty, she'd decided she needed an unofficial option. And Jacob

Powell, ex-Special Forces airstrike pilot and current high-stakes bounty hunter was about as unofficial as it got.

More importantly, from what she'd heard over the years—not that she'd been keeping tabs on him, of course—having him on her side was like having an entire private army at her disposal. That, more than anything, had compelled her to make the drive to the bounty hunters' headquarters in the mountains. If she could have avoided this awkward reunion, she would have. But duty—and failure—had made it a necessity.

So she opened her eyes and shoved herself upright on the couch in one smooth move that left her head reeling and her stomach fisting on a slap of nausea.

God, she hated percussion bombs. She'd caught the edge of a relatively mild flash-bang during training and her ears had rung for a week. The one in the chalet had nearly flattened her. Then LBJ had finished the job with one blow of a gun butt.

By the time she'd come to, it had all been over. Secretary Cooper had been unconscious, tied to a dining room chair.

And Hope and the twin girls had been gone.

Kidnapped.

"Isabella." Jacob's voice softened on the word, sending a spear of pain straight through her chest. "Talk to me."

Because he was why she'd turned away from the airport and headed into the hills, she opened her eyes. And nearly closed them again.

He stood across the small office, shifting from foot

to foot. When she'd thought of him over the years—and she'd thought of him as little as possible—her memories had been of constant motion and unflinching intensity. That hadn't changed.

But other parts of him had. He was bigger than she remembered. Not taller, though at five-eleven, he'd always topped her by a good four inches, but broader. More solid. More muscular—and the Jacob she remembered had been plenty muscular to begin with.

Remembering those muscles, and the masculine skin that covered them, she twisted to put her feet on the floor, clutching the edge of the leather-covered sofa cushion for balance.

Jacob frowned. "You should stay down. You're pretty banged up."

"I'm fine." In reality, she had a hell of a headache, but Cooper had begged her not to alert the resort's medical staff. She glanced at Jacob. "I need your help."

He stilled. "What happened?"

She fought the urge to close her eyes again, to block out the things she'd seen once she'd regained consciousness. The quiet chalet. Louis Cooper tied to a dining room chair with a message written across his naked chest in his own blood.

Images of failure. Of danger. Of a possible national crisis in the making that she was forbidden to speak of.

But damn it, she wasn't going to let something like this happen. Not on her watch.

So she kept her eyes level on his and saw his body vibrate with the need to pace, to do something. Or maybe that was her body? How could she be this near him after all these years and not feel the pull?

She couldn't. That was the simple answer. Just looking at him warmed her stomach and tightened her throat, and not only from the memories, but from his sheer presence. He seemed to fill the office, dominate it, possess it. If she could have turned and run, she would have. But Hope and the girls needed her help and Jacob was her only hope, damn it.

She took a breath, swallowed and said, "Louis Cooper's family was abducted from the Golf Resort five hours ago."

The sentence crushed her, as though saying it out loud made it more real. She half expected Jacob to shout at her, to panic, to tell her she was no damn good—because that was what she'd told herself, and that was the hair-trigger temper she remembered.

But he merely nodded and watched her from across the room. "Tell me everything."

Something broke inside her, loosening the band around her heart. She almost told him how gut-wrenchingly, mind numbingly scared she'd been when she'd seen Louis Cooper's body tied to a chair, limp and covered with blood.

She, who was never, ever, scared.

But telling him that would be leaning. Leeching. All those needy, greedy things he'd accused her of when they'd broken up and she'd realized that the things she'd seen as togetherness, as love, he'd seen as her being controlling. Clinging. Unstable.

Like her mother.

And, blast it, where had that come from? That whole mess was ancient history.

Isabella jammed her eyelids down, scrubbed vicious circles along her temples and shoved the memories clear out of her mind. She was a different person now. *He* was a different person. They couldn't come at this from where they'd been back then. They needed to start fresh. Special Agent to local law, though he wasn't technically the law.

Hopefully, he was still interested in justice.

"I was assigned to protect Secretary Cooper. He and his family have been threatened because of the Lunkinburg situation." She glanced over and saw by Jacob's faint nod that he followed the politics. He was standing across the room, back to the door as though he wanted to be anywhere else. The index finger of his left hand—he was ambidextrous in all ways that counted, she remembered with a faint wash of heat—twitched against his thigh. The rest of him was still, though leashed energy vibrated in the room.

His constant need for motion used to exhaust her, annoy her. Now she found it a comfort. If she could harness all that energy—

"If you were attacked five hours ago and Cooper's family taken, the sooner you tell me—or the authorities—what happened, the better. The chances of finding abductees decrease exponentially with time." His expression didn't waver. It was locked between coolness and dismissal, both of which seemed at odds with what she remembered from that first moment their eyes had met downstairs. She'd felt the click of recognition, the hard wash of heat, and she'd seen the same flare in his expression, the same moment of hope, then memory.

What did it mean?

Nothing. It meant nothing. She wasn't here to rekindle a former romance that had ended bloodily. She was here because she had no other option. Because Hope and the girls needed her.

"You're right." She took a deep breath, organized her uncharacteristically scattered thoughts and made her report, pretending she was speaking to one of her bosses rather than to her ex-lover. "Not long after the press conference, maybe five-thirty this afternoon, Secretary Cooper's chalet at the Golf Resort was attacked. A percussion bomb stunned the occupants of the chalet." *Including me,* she wanted to say, but didn't because it was easier to report things this way.

She strove for the professional detachment she prided herself on, the lack of emotion so different from who she'd been, where she'd come from. "Three men entered the chalet wearing rubber masks resembling Presidents Nixon, Johnson and Clinton." She pulled out the mental snapshot she'd taken of the attackers and compared them to each other, to the furniture and walls. Remembered them coming toward her. "Nixon was about five-ten and skinny as a rail. Mid-brown hair on his arms and hands. Johnson and Clinton were taller and more muscular, though still lean."

She paused, remembering the blow, the unconsciousness and the screaming fear of coming around and not knowing what she would find.

Of finding three of her four protectees gone.

When Jacob remained quiet, motionless except for his left index finger, which continued to tap a complicated beat against his leg, she continued. "They…" She swallowed, realizing she couldn't give the report from a distance now. "I missed with my first shot, hit Nixon in the leg and got off two more rounds before they rendered me unconscious." There, that sounded more detached than *clubbed me with a gun butt,* more professional than *knocked me out.*

Being professional and unemotional was the key here.

She thought Jacob muttered something, but when she looked at him, the cool expression was firmly in place. "Go on," he said. "Time's wasting."

No kidding. She could feel the minutes and hours slipping by as though they hid beneath her skin. So she plowed through the rest of the story and tried to put her mind on hold. "When I came to, the three men were gone. Secretary Cooper was tied to a chair, unconscious. They probably used chloroform, by the smell of it." She sucked in a breath and said the rest in a rush. "His wife, Hope, and twin toddlers, Becky and Tiffany, were gone. I revived and untied him, but before I could search the premises, the Secretary directed me to play the answering machine back. There was a message."

She paused and wrestled with the memory. No matter how far she detached herself, the low, gritty voice and the feeling of absolute failure cut through her defenses.

Jacob's finger stilled. "Keep going."

"The voice—male, no discernable accent—stated that Secretary Cooper's family was safe for now, but would be killed if the kidnappers' instructions were not followed to the letter." She searched back, trying to remember the exact phrasing and intonation. "If Secretary Cooper alerted the authorities, his wife and daughters would die. Additional instructions would follow." She remembered the beat of silence that had followed the kidnappers' message, the absolute horror in Louis Cooper's eyes, the cold spear of guilt in her heart. She swallowed. "That was all."

"Did you follow the instructions?" Jacob asked, his whole body tense with its stillness.

"I wouldn't have," she admitted. "I wanted to call my superiors and the FBI immediately, but Secretary Cooper forbade it." His eyes had been wild, his grip on her wrist too strong to deny. Nearly maniacal in his support of the U.S. policy against negotiating with terrorists, Louis Cooper had crumbled at the threat to his young family. Not that she could blame him. The very thought of sweet Hope and the two eighteen-month old girls in captivity was enough to make her want to weep. Or scream.

"And you listened to him?" The faint bite underlying Jacob's words scratched along Isabella's nerve endings like an accusation.

"I had no choice," she snapped. "He called my superiors and had me removed from duty. I'm off the active list until my next assignment starts in a month."

And that was the cruelest cut of all. Though she was one of the most effective agents in the D.C. field office, she knew she wasn't particularly popular. She just didn't get how some of her co-workers turned their personalities on and off, how they went from goofy pranksters or sensitive touchy-feely types to hard-nosed agents in an instant. She couldn't do that—it came too close to what she'd grown up with, a mother who was on top of the world one day, in the dregs of despair the next. Because of it, she'd gotten the reputation of being effective but not particularly friendly. All about the job. And if the labels had stung, she'd shoved the feelings aside because they were, after all, only feelings.

She knew that if it had been one of the other agents being shoved off the secretary's protection detail, the bosses would have asked questions. But because it was her, the field office had shrugged and made the change.

Tears prickled out of nowhere and she catapulted from the couch to pace, not realizing until it was too late that her path between a set of wooden shelves and a paper-covered desk would bring her dangerously close to Jacob.

He grabbed her arms. The feel of his strong fingers raced through her like lightning and she reeled back, tried to break free from the heat and temptation.

"Isabella!" He shook her gently. "Iz, I know you're hurt. I know you're tired and shocky, but you've got to do better than this. Why didn't you go to your superiors yourself? Why did you come here?"

How did you know where I was? The question hung unasked between them, but there was no way she was answering. He didn't need to know that she checked up on him now and then, didn't need to know that she'd tried to duck the Montana assignment, not wanting to be in the same state as the Big Sky Bounty Hunters' headquarters.

Most of all, he didn't need to know she had measured every man in her life since college against him and found them lacking in everything except kindness.

Because whatever Jacob Powell was, he wasn't kind.

But she wasn't looking for kindness now. She needed a warrior, and he fit the bill.

She pulled away from him and crossed her arms to form a pitiful shield between them. "Louis Cooper's report to my superiors took care of that. He's smart, he knew exactly how to make it sound like I'd gone mentally shaky and he was trying to cover for me. Thus, the month off."

And that had galled her down to the bone. But her mother's problems were in her record, and the condition was genetic. Add that to her reputation as slightly antisocial, and *wham*.

Instant paid suspension pending a psych eval. Even the thought fisted her stomach with memory and dread. But she didn't have time for that garbage. Cooper's family was out there somewhere and she was damn well going to find them.

"So why are you here?" Jacob asked again, his closed expression brooking no evasions.

"I need help." It stung to admit it, but there was more. "And I think you'll be interested in hearing who took Hope and the girls."

"They left a name?"

"No." She shook her head. "A calling card of sorts.

Until I saw it, I thought the attack was linked to the Lunkinburg issue and the stand-up Cooper did with Prince Nikolai."

"Logical enough," Jacob agreed. "King Aleksandr's statement after that press conference certainly wasn't friendly." His tone sharpened. "But you don't think so now?"

She wasn't quite sure what to think. It didn't add up. "I said they left a calling card. A signature, in fact, drawn in Cooper's own blood across his chest." She glanced over at Jacob, found his eyes intent on her. "MMFAFA."

Jacob's disbelief vibrated between them for a split second, then he was in motion. He yanked the door open and bellowed, "Everyone to the situation room, now!" Then he slammed the door and spun toward her, eyes alight with excitement and a hint of accusation. "That's our bounty. The Montana Militia for a Free America. Eight members of the group escaped from The Fortress last month and we've been on their trail ever since. If this is their work…" He trailed off, spun and yanked the door open. "Stay here."

She grabbed his arm and felt him stiffen even as the sizzle of heat raced through her body at the contact. "I want in on this. I know your group was involved with the MMFAFA incident with the train derailment, and I know your bounty is still at large. We can help each other. Why else do you think I came here?"

He shrugged her off. "Because you didn't have any-place else to go." She stepped back, stung, and he cursed at himself. "Sorry, that was nasty. And I'm grateful you brought me this information. But you have no idea who you're dealing with here—it'd be best if you stay here while we take care of it. These men are dangerous. Violent."

She grabbed his arm again when he tried to leave the room, and this time hung on when he brushed her off. She kept her voice low and urgent. "I'm a Secret Service agent, and a damned good one. You think I haven't gone up against militias before? That I can't handle myself in dangerous situations? Well, to hell with you. I'm in this thing all the way." When he glanced down at her fingers on his arm and raised one eyebrow, rage flared and she snapped. "Don't you dare accuse me of clinging or being irrational. It was my job to protect Louis Cooper. My *duty*. There's no way I'm letting you take over. Not while there's breath in my body."

Jacob froze, even the background sparks of motion stilling as his eyes went dark. Isabella expected an explosion.

Instead his voice softened. "I wasn't going to accuse you of being irrational." He took a breath, then said, "I'm sorry about how I handled things back at Georgetown. You weren't clingy or irrational, or any of the things I accused you of. You wanted a ring and I wanted an out, so I hit you where I knew it would hurt most." Even as his words slashed through the years around her heart, his voice hardened again. "But that's ancient history and this is today. I don't want you anywhere near Boone and his maniac followers. Stay here and let us do our jobs."

He squeezed her hand, removed it from his arm and slipped through the door.

Isabella saw it shut, heard a dead bolt slide and realized there was a lock on either side. Some office.

But even as her mind noted these details, her consciousness grappled with Jacob's words. Perhaps it was way too little and thirteen years too late, but his apology left her shaken. It brought back a lurking tendril of graduation day when she'd accused him of being unfaithful and he'd thrown it right back at her, saying she had pushed him away with the very closeness she had so depended on, so wanted.

I'm sorry. His words echoed in her heart. *I hit you where I knew it would hurt most.* For a girl whose goal was to break free from her upbringing to hear that she'd gone right back there—

Yeah, it had hurt.

"But that's neither here nor there," she said out loud, wincing when her voice scraped on the words. "What's important now is rescuing Cooper's family."

And there was no way she was leaving that solely to Jacob and his teammates, she thought, determination hardening in her soul. No way in hell.

She tried the door to confirm it was locked, then scanned the room. The desk held a nifty computer locked in wait mode—though she was pretty sure she could crack it if she took the time—and news printouts with cryptic notes in the margins. There were no photographs or personal items, but the air smelled of Jacob.

So why did he have locks on both sides of his door?

Masculine voices rose from downstairs, likely shock

and excitement as Jacob revealed that the bounty hunters' quarry had been involved in abducting the Secretary of Defense's family.

Gritting her teeth with the need to be out there making her report, Isabella turned to the single small window. It wasn't locked, but a bar prevented it from opening more than halfway. The gap was too small for a man to pass through.

But she was no man.

JACOB SCANNED the faces of the half dozen bounty hunters assembled in the situation room on the lower level of the headquarters. Away from the public eye, the "basement" contained a warren of interconnected rooms boasting weapons, interrogation rooms and more surveillance equipment than most Secret Service field offices.

Although Cameron Murphy was their leader, the former Special Forces colonel gestured for Jacob to proceed with the meeting. "Why don't you fill us in on our mystery lady upstairs?"

"Agent Isabella Gray." Preternaturally aware of the zing in his blood from where she'd touched him, Jacob cleared his throat, shoved his hands into his pockets to keep them from twitching, and paced. "She was in charge of protecting the Secretary of Defense, Louis Cooper. Near dinnertime, three masked men disabled Agent Gray and Secretary Cooper with a flash-bang and kidnapped his wife and twin girls. A message on the answering machine warned of a ransom demand to follow."

He grimaced. Saying the words out loud punched him below the heart. He might have learned long ago that just as he wasn't going to be the son his parents wanted, he also wasn't marriage-and-babies material. But the thought of a man's family being taken brought a fierce spurt of anger. Quickly he sketched in the rest of the attack and the circumstances of Isabella's suspension, ending with, "She says Cooper had letters written across his chest. MMFAFA."

There was a collective hiss of indrawn breath. A quiet oath, though Jacob wasn't sure who had cursed. He nodded. "Yeah. Boone Fowler and his boys are at it again. This might be just the break we need to catch these bastards."

"Is Agent Gray going to be involved?" The question came from Mike Clark. Tall and lanky, brown-haired and brown-eyed, Mike read body language like it was vernacular English, which Jacob found vaguely creepy.

He shifted, wondering what Mike saw in him, what his body said about his relationship with Isabella. "She's given me all the information she has. She'll be safe here while we track the bounty."

Cameron frowned. "She has training and experience, and if Cooper and his family were under her protection, she has major motivation to go after the kidnappers. You don't think we should use her?"

"No, sir, I don't," Jacob said flatly. "She stays in my office. Period."

At that moment he didn't care what Mike was reading off his body language. He only cared that Isabella be kept as far away from Boone Fowler as possible.

Fowler and his men had killed hundreds of innocents over the years. They had killed Cameron's sister five years earlier and shot Cameron in the shoulder. The leader of Big Sky Bounty Hunters still carried a scar and a grudge. Since their escape from The Fortress, the militiamen had murdered at least two others—a German diplomat and the governor of Montana.

Jacob would be damned if they got to Isabella.

A brisk knock at the door of the situation room interrupted his train of thought and had Cameron reaching for the lockdown button beneath the conference table.

Suspicion prickled at Jacob and he held up a hand. "Wait." He reached over and flicked on the surveillance cams monitoring the hall. "Well, I'll be damned."

Isabella stood outside the door, hands on her hips and a determined look on her bruised face as she stared up into the camera. A hidden microphone picked up her words. "Don't even think you're keeping me out of this, Jacob Powell."

His quick surprise was followed by a spike of temper. He yanked the door open, pulled her inside and banged the door shut. "How did you get out of—" He scrubbed a hand through his hair. "You climbed out the *window?* You're insane. You realize that, don't you? You're insane!"

It wasn't until he saw her flinch that he realized what he'd said and cursed himself inwardly. But just as the heat between them had always flared near uncontrollable bounds, he instantly aimed to wound when it came to her. He opened his mouth to apologize—again—but Cameron nudged him aside.

"Cameron Murphy." He stuck out a hand. "I'm the boss around here, and Boone Fowler, leader of the MM-FAFA, is my bounty." His tone brooked no argument. "Big Sky is collaborating with the authorities on tracking the fugitives and we'd appreciate any information you could give us."

Isabella shook hands with him, her expression tinged with wariness as she scanned the assembly. All ex-Special Forces, the bounty hunters were an intimidating lot.

But she stuck out her chin as though leading for a punch, and said, "I help you, you help me. Quid pro quo."

"Meaning?" Cam asked mildly while Jacob shifted from foot to foot, suppressing the urge to toss her over his shoulder, carry her back to his office and lock the window, bar the door, and nail the whole thing tight.

"Meaning I'll give you what I have and what I know, but I want in on the search. I'm quick, smart, trained, and I have a hell of a motivation. Louis Cooper, his wife and baby girls are my responsibility. That doesn't stop just because the kidnappers have convinced him to block my official abilities."

"Don't do it," Jacob said to his boss in a near growl, though he'd never dared tell Cam what to do before. "You know what Fowler and his men are like. What about your sister's death? What about when Fowler almost killed your wife?"

The other men shifted and glanced at each other, obviously expecting Cam to blast Jacob. But instead the Big Sky leader said mildly, "Agent Gray isn't my sister. Like Mia, she's trained, and unless I miss my guess, Isabella has a weapon tucked at the small of her back. That goes a long way toward leveling sexual prejudices in my book. And—" his look was less forgiving than his tone "—if Mia ever heard you say that, she'd kick your ass. Don't forget she was a bounty hunter when we hooked up."

"That's neither here nor there." Jacob's fingers worried a plastic dart flight in his pocket. "I don't want Isabella involved."

"I get that." Cam turned to Isabella. "Without knowing what is—or was—between you and Powell, let me ask. Are you going to have a problem working with him?"

Expression flat, she shook her head. "Not on your life. Whatever was between us died a long, long time ago. Now it's just leftovers, and I can deal with leftovers."

Ouch. Jacob's temper flared even before Cam cut a glance in his direction and asked, "How about you?"

She's nuts, he wanted to say. *Leftovers my butt.* But over the years he'd thought long and hard about what he'd done to her, what he'd said, and he'd realized that cruelty was cruelty, whatever the provocation. And he tried not to be a cruel man.

So instead he fisted his hands in his pockets and felt the dart flight crumple into a ball. "No problem whatsoever, boss. It'll be just like working with one of the guys."

"Fine then." Cam extended his hand for a second shake. "Welcome to the team, Special Agent Gray. Now, let's get to work."

But as the bounty hunters—plus one suspended Secret Service agent—sat around the conference table, Jacob knew it was anything but fine. He didn't want Isabella near Boone Fowler and his followers.

And he'd be damned if he was a leftover.

Chapter Three

An hour later Isabella, Jacob and two other bounty hunt-ers headed to the Golf Resort for a recon. She let Jacob drive her rented Jeep, not because she'd felt particularly shaky, but because she'd lacked the energy to argue when he insisted.

And because the situation was so damned weird.

In the first few years after she and Jacob had gone their separate ways, one part of her had hated him like poison while another had dreamed of their reunion, how he would one day realize they'd had something special together, something he couldn't find with any-one else.

Unfortunately the reverse had been true. Over the months and years, Isabella's hatred had dimmed and she'd come to realize that he'd been right about some of the things he'd said. They'd been too young, their re-lationship too intense to do anything but burn itself out. She'd forgiven him for that, but not for the way he'd ended it, the way he'd gotten drunk, picked a fight, picked up a girl, and the next day tried to blame it all on her.

He'd faded from her conscious mind as she progressed from the Criminal Investigations Training Program in Georgia to the Secret Service Training Academy in Maryland. By the time she'd gotten herself established in her first field office, Jacob had become little more than a memory of the all-consuming, scary emotions that she tried like hell to avoid.

And she had. For almost thirteen years she'd avoided emotional hot flashes and brain-scrambling entanglements. She'd built herself a solid, steady life. It wasn't predictable—how could the Protections Division ever be that?—and it wasn't always safe—but the danger she'd encountered had always came from without, never within.

Until now.

When she'd made the decision to drive to the Big Sky headquarters, she'd told herself she could handle seeing Jacob again. But she wasn't sure she could handle the wild emotions that had bubbled to the surface the moment she'd seen him, the moment she'd touched him.

She was supposed to have outgrown those feelings, damn it.

"Your head bothering you?"

She jolted at the sound of his voice, then consciously smoothed out her frown. "No. It's fine." She pointed at a passing sign. "Turn in here, the resort is a mile and a half up on the left. Use the second entrance. Secretary Cooper stayed in the Presidential Chalet."

Which was sadly ironic, given that men wearing ex-presidents' faces had taken his family.

"No problem." He threaded the Jeep through the winding roads as though he knew exactly where he was going.

Which he probably did, she realized with faint discomfort. He'd lived in the area for close to five years now, and undoubtedly knew these roads better than she did.

But he hadn't snapped when she'd bossed him with the directions. He would have before, she thought, then cursed under her breath. She needed to stop comparing the Jacob of today with the one she'd known in college.

"Problem?" His single word settled between them, asking so many more things than it should have.

She let out a frustrated breath. "Yeah. Problem. But it's my problem, not yours."

He followed the signs toward the chalet where Secretary Cooper and his family had stayed. Isabella shivered when they passed between the monstrous stone pillars edged with copper filigree. At Jacob's sharp look, she shrugged. "The last time I turned through here, Secretary Cooper was playing patty-cake with one of the girls in the back of the limo. Hope and I were chatting about the area. It was normal. Relaxed." Or as relaxed as she allowed herself to be on the job.

Jacob parked the Jeep in front of the chalet and waited while the SUV containing the other bounty hunters parked off to the side. Then he turned, looked at her too closely and said, "It wasn't your fault, Isabella."

Something shifted in her chest and her eyes burned. She wanted to lean into him, to crawl against him. Weakness. He was her weakness, the man who brought tricky emotions too near the surface and made her want to burrow in and cling.

Hating the frailty, the temptation, she climbed out of the Jeep and slammed the door hard enough to attract the attention of the other bounty hunters. Rather than explain—especially since she couldn't even explain it to herself—she said, "Right after he relieved me of my duties, Secretary Cooper made arrangements to return to Washington. The cleaning crew won't be in until tomorrow, so everything should be undisturbed. But I didn't find anything in the quick run-through I was able to make before Cooper kicked me out, and I'll bet he picked the place up so there wouldn't be any suspicion. He's committed to doing everything the kidnappers have demanded, particularly keeping the authorities out of this."

It tugged at her that a man of Cooper's stature and conviction could be so badly compromised by a threat to his family. A threat that never should have come to pass.

"Let's get on with it." A dark-haired, heavily muscled hunter named Tony hefted a case that looked like a souped-up crime scene field kit. "We need to be in and out before dawn."

Isabella nodded shortly. "Come on." She unlocked the front door with her key and pushed into the chalet before the hesitation could form. She didn't want to look at the bullet-stung sofa and imagine Hope and the girls, didn't want to look at the dining room table, hastily righted and reorganized, and remember seeing Louis Cooper bound to a chair, unmoving. But it was those images that, hopefully, would provide a clue.

Mike and Tony moved into the chalet for a preliminary sweep. They didn't touch anything right away, instead getting an overall feeling of the scene of the crime, which should have had technicians swarming over it with state-of-the-art equipment instead of one lame duck agent and three bounty hunters.

Isabella felt an uncharacteristic, unwelcome press of tears at how quickly this had gone down, how completely her work—and Louis Cooper's life—had been derailed. She swallowed hard and flinched when Jacob touched her arm.

She glanced at him and saw that his eyes asked, *Are you okay?* But out loud, he said, "How did they get in? Break a window in the back?"

"No." The bitter failure of it burned her throat. "I looked. They didn't break a damned thing. One minute everything was fine and the next they were inside my perimeter setting off a flash-bang in the living room. How?" She spread her hands to indicate confusion. Anger churned in her gut. "Damned if I know. I had the locks changed last week, and motions set around the far perimeter. They shouldn't have been able to get through."

He stared past her as the two other bounty hunters moved from room to room, turning on the lights as they went. The illumination lent a strangely cheerful glow to the empty space. "Maybe they got the new keys from someone on the inside," Jacob said.

"Probably. Damn it." Isabella forced herself to move into the dining room and look around, though she'd done so not seven hours earlier while Secretary Cooper had made his travel arrangements with shaking hands, then made a second call that effectively cut her off at the knees by subtly claiming she'd been acting irrational.

Irrational, my ass.

She felt the old, familiar anger and gritted her teeth. "Fine. Let's do this."

They searched the chalet from top to bottom, but Cooper had been thorough. He'd removed the tape from the old-fashioned answering machine, wiped the flash-bang soot off the walls and even flipped the torn leather cushion, which set off soft warning bells in the back of her mind.

It seemed like awfully clear thinking for a man whose family had been kidnapped.

But what was the alternative? That the kidnappers had come back afterward to clean the chalet? Unlikely.

So, senses heightened, she moved from room to room, searching again and watching the men of Big Sky perform a thorough forensic scan. Cameron Murphy's bounty hunters had the reputation of being the best at what they did—and their skills were many and varied.

Not that she'd checked them out, or anything.

Then again, who was she kidding? She was preternaturally aware of Jacob's every move, his quiet words to the others.

And that just ticked her off more. No doubt he hadn't spared her another thought after they split. He certainly hadn't tried to get in touch over the years.

Cursing inwardly, she redirected her thoughts, tossed

the bedroom as thoroughly as she could, and sucked in a breath when she unearthed a squeaky duck from behind the bureau. It was purple, which meant it was Tiffany's. The twins were nearly identical in looks and attitude, but Tiff loved purple and Becky preferred yellow.

God, she thought, *please let them be okay.*

She wanted to throw the cheerful little duck against the wall and howl at the injustice. She wanted to cuddle it close and pray for the babies and their mother.

Instead she set the toy on the bed and kept searching.

"I'VE GOT NOTHING." Jacob glanced over his shoulder at Mike, who was meticulously dusting the door handle that lead out to the back porch. "You?"

"Wiped clean." The normally garrulous Clark straightened from his task with an it's-late-and-I'm-tired groan. "This is a bust. Let's get your woman and get out of here."

"She's not my woman," Jacob snapped with a quick, vicious bite of temper toward a man he considered a friend—if a slightly creepy one.

"If you say so." Mike shrugged, but his eyes were sharp on Jacob's face. On his stance.

"And don't try to read me, either," Jacob growled. "I'm not a suspect."

"I don't *try* to read anyone, I read them. And do you want to know what I see right now? I see—"

"No!" Jacob leaned down and got in the other man's face. "I absolutely don't want to know. I don't believe in that hocus-pocus cr—"

"Jacob?" Isabella said from behind him. "Am I interrupting?"

He spun toward the arched doorway and the anger morphed again, this time into something hot and greedy. Something he hadn't felt in a long, long time and didn't welcome. "Yes, damn it, you're—" *Interrupting,* he started to say but made himself bite the words off.

It wasn't her fault he couldn't deal with seeing her again. But just as seeing her on the television screen had immediately jarred him out of whack, having her an arm's length away was…too tempting.

He was trying to handle it. Damn it, he *was* handling it. But he wasn't handling the quick return of his oldest enemy—anger. He hated that she'd brought back that same sense of being trapped, of being out of control.

God, he hated this. And it wasn't even her fault. Hell, from the looks of her, cool as a Montana stream, she wasn't feeling a tenth of what he was. Which made it his problem, not hers.

So he took a breath and leveled his tone. "No, you're not interrupting. We're finished in here. We've got nothing. You?"

She shook her head and her auburn hair followed the motion in a slide of color and softness. "I didn't find anything, but Tony wants you two at the back door."

"Let's go." Glad to have something to do, Jacob gestured for her to go first, a bit of manners ingrained by his mother—or rather by the fleet of nannies, dance instructors and protocol experts she'd hired to shape her son into a civilized man like his father.

It had all been another level of control, one he'd gloried at escaping in college and broken free of just after, though he'd left a part of himself behind.

And wasn't sure how to get it back. Wasn't sure he wanted to.

Yet at the same time, the mossy-eyed woman with the rich auburn hair pulled at him, made him want to be a different man than the one he'd made himself. Because he didn't know how to deal with that, or with her, he ignored Isabella to crouch beside Tony in the foyer just inside the back door. "What have you got?"

The lean, black-haired bounty hunter used the blunt end of a scoopula—a tool that had a sharp blade on one end, a small rounded scoop on the other—to scrape a clump of dirt off the rattan mat. "Maybe nothing. But maybe something. I'm betting the latter."

"Tell me." Jacob gestured for Mike to join him and stiffened when Isabella elbowed her way into the huddle.

"Look at it very closely." Tony held the small metal scoop up to the artificial light coming from an elegant chandelier above them. "What do you see?"

Jacob squinted. "Dirt?"

"Not just dirt." Isabella pressed closer to the sample, nearly leaning across Jacob's lap. "There's something else in there. Something green?"

Jacob gritted his teeth and tried like hell not to breathe, but her scent enveloped him, swamped him, surprised him. It was nothing like the flowers-and-sunshine perfume he remembered from before. This was a woman's scent, sharp and spicy and take-no-prisoners.

Like Isabella herself.

"Exactly," Tony said. "That's oxidized copper ore you're seeing, which means…"

Isabella leaned even closer, so her upper arm and the side of one breast pressed against Jacob's shoulder. He ground his teeth and shifted away as she said, "Which means it could have come from one of the mining areas." She sat back, frowning, and Jacob took a breath that was tainted with her essence, even though she wasn't crowding his space anymore. "But how does that help us? There are hundreds of mines in this state."

"True." Tony smiled, his too handsome face folding into creases and dimples that never failed to attract the ladies.

Knowing it, and knowing Tony's love-'em-and-leave-'em philosophy, Jacob angled his body between Isabella and the other bounty hunter and snarled, "So why are you grinning like this dirt is a clue?"

"Because," Tony answered easily, "I've got degrees in geology and topology. I know my dirt. Copper was only mined in one area of the state, about two hours north of here. There are maybe a half dozen shafts, all within short drives of each other."

"You think it's worth chasing dirt?" Mike asked dubiously. "What if Cooper brought it in on his shoes? Or maybe one of the security folks? No offense, Agent Gray." He nodded at Isabella.

She shrugged. "It's Isabella, and no offense taken. But I can guarantee it wasn't from the secretary or his family—they haven't gone sight-seeing since we arrived. Hope…" Jacob saw her swallow after the name, but when she spoke again, her voice was firm. Unemotional. "Hope preferred to shop. And it wasn't the local cops. They weren't allowed in the chalet. I was the only one on internal security."

Tony cut his gaze back to Mike. "So our best guess is that the dirt came along with the kidnappers. And if the kidnappers really do represent the MMFAFA…"

"Then our bounty could be hiding in or near one of these copper mines." Jacob felt the beginning of a connection form in his brain. The beginnings of excitement. Hell, they might be onto something here.

"Bingo." Tony dumped the sample into a small screw-top jar. "So the way I see it, we need to do two things. One, we head over to the mine area—it'll be dawn by the time we get there—and search as many as we can. Maybe we'll get lucky. If not, we can take samples from each site and I'll run some basic comparisons. Once we've identified where the fugitives have been, we can plant some surveillance equipment."

"Good idea." Mike straightened to his feet. "Vermin usually return to their burrows."

Jacob stood, as well, and offered Isabella a hand with his family's good manners. She ignored him and rose unassisted. He scowled and told himself to focus on the job. Which reminded him of something. "And don't forget about the break-in at the clinic."

When the other bounty hunters turned to stare, he cursed. How could he have forgotten about that?

Isabella had arrived, that was how. Since the first moment he'd seen her that evening he'd been running on half a brain, with the other half stuck in *remember when* mode. Or, more honestly, *remember when* combined with a healthy dose of lust that had very little to do with past history and everything to do with the fact that Isabella had grown from a hot college babe to a striking woman who still had the power to unglue his brain.

And if he'd resented the power she had over him thirteen years earlier, he mistrusted it even more now. He was a grown man. She didn't have the right to make him feel this way.

Yet in fairness, she had done nothing untoward. It was all him. His weakness. His anger. His lack of control.

"Jacob? You said something about a clinic?" Her husky voice cut through the confusion.

"Sorry." He took a breath and forced himself to focus on the job. On his bounty. That was what he was now, a bounty hunter. He was proud of the work, and as an added bonus, his parents remained genteelly horrified by his career choice. "I e-mailed a friend over at the dispatcher's office earlier tonight, to see if she had news on the fugitives. She said one of the local walk-in clinics was tossed earlier this evening. You add that to Isabella's report that she shot one of the kidnappers in the leg, and we might have something."

"You're darned right we might." Tony clapped Jacob on the shoulder nearly hard enough to send him flying. "Let's head for the mines. I don't think there's anything else to see here."

When the other men gathered their kits and headed for the front door, Jacob hung back. "You guys go ahead and update the others. I'm going to take Isabella to headquarters for some rest. I'll meet you out at the mines."

"The hell you will!" She rounded on him. "You've already been outvoted once on this issue. Do we really need to discuss it again? Like it or not, I'm working with you on this case. Let's face it, you wouldn't even have these leads if I hadn't brought them to you."

"That's right." Jacob scowled and stepped in until he could feel her body heat. "But let's also not forget that you came to me. You're cut off, discredited and counting on us for help. So you could try being a bit more cooperative." She paled at his words and Jacob cursed inwardly. What was it about her that made him so mean?

Fighting the urge to grab on and shake some sense into her, he softened his voice, though he was acutely aware of the others listening with avid interest. "Be reasonable, Iz. You've had a hell of a day. You're bruised, battered and probably concussed. And how much sleep have you gotten in the last couple of days? It can't have been easy arranging the protection solo." He continued before she could snap back at him. "You need rest and aspirin. You need to shut it off for a few hours, or you'll be no good to us or to your protectees."

He saw the war in her eyes, the need to dig her heels in fighting with the logic.

Logic finally won. Her shoulders slumped and she sighed. "You're right. I know you're right, but I don't like it."

"Nobody said you had to." Jacob jerked his head at

Mike and Tony, sending them on their way, and resisted the urge to reach out to Isabella when she leaned against the wall and closed her eyes.

"Every time I slow down, every time I blink, I see Hope and the girls. I see the look in Louis Cooper's eyes when he woke up and realized they were gone. The expression on his face when he heard that message." She pushed away from the wall. "But you're right. I need to grab a few hours." Her lips curved. "You won't even need to lock me in while you and the others search the mines. I'll sleep a bit on your couch, then call in a few favors I'm owed by people who might not have heard about my suspension yet."

"Sounds like a plan." He gestured her toward the front door and turned off the remainder of the interior lights. "And, Isabella?"

"Yes?" She paused just inside the front door and turned back to him. The outdoor light cast her in shadow, emphasizing the bruise on her cheek and the dark circles beneath her eyes that made her look young. Vulnerable. Sad.

He shrugged and felt his clothes bind as though they didn't fit quite right. *I'm glad you came to me,* he wanted to say, because it scared him to think of her out there alone, searching for Boone Fowler and his men, who would skin her as soon as look at her.

Because of that fear, and because he was suddenly swamped with the irrational desire to pull her into his arms and tell her everything was going to be okay, he scowled and jammed his hands into his pockets. "Never mind. Let's get out of here. We can send someone back tomorrow to question the staff. There had to be an insider with access to the keys and the security system."

She nodded and slipped through the front door as though grateful to be away from the emptiness of the chalet. He couldn't blame her. It was damned eerie how all that violence had been wiped away with a hasty cleaning.

Feeling a small shiver prickle the nape of his neck, Jacob snapped off the last light to plunge them into deep darkness. He closed the front door, which locked behind them, and shivered for real as the September cold sliced through his leather jacket.

It might still be pleasant during the day, but the nights were getting harsher. Snow was on the way. Winter.

"Brr." Isabella rubbed warmth into her arms. At least he thought she did. In the deep night before dawn, he barely saw the motion, though the cold and the dark seemed to amplify the sound of rustling cloth and the whisper of skin over skin.

"Here." He shrugged out of his jacket and draped it over her shoulders, which were just barely visible as a lighter shape against the dark. He probably should have left the front light on, but they'd wanted to leave the chalet as they had found it—abandoned. "Don't argue," he said sharply when she protested. "Just take it, okay? It's freezing."

She was quiet a moment, then simply said, "Thank you."

He wasn't sure why, but it felt like a major victory, though now the cold bit through his shirt and sank down to the bone. "Come on. Let's get back to headquarters."

The short path to the parking area was open, lit with a fitful slice of light from a streetlamp at the end of the drive. Stone crunched beneath their feet and Jacob moved closer to Isabella, more from instinct than desire.

He walked her to the passenger side of the Jeep, opened the door to hand her in—

And something moved in the brush nearby.

"Get in!" Knowing his gun was locked in the glove compartment, he yanked the gun from Isabella's mid-back holster and pushed her into the Jeep. Cursing himself for assuming the scene was safe, he spun toward the noise thinking it might be a grizzly bear, but quickly realized that the noise was two-legged and receding with distance.

Someone had been watching the chalet. Watching them.

"Chase him, you idiot!" Isabella was past Jacob in a flash. She raced across the short stretch of lawn and plunged into the dense forest in pursuit.

Unarmed.

Heart pounding, gut clenched hard enough to tell him this was a really, really bad idea, Jacob sprinted after her, following the noise of crashing brush and footfalls when his dark-adapted sight failed him.

"Isabella, slow down," he hissed, doubting she could hear him, but not wanting to advertise that a woman was in the lead.

But she heard. Without pausing, she called back, "I've almost got him. I've—"

Jacob heard a horrible crash. A scream.

Then silence.

Chapter Four

Isabella had been sure her quarry was up ahead, so when the man came out of the inky darkness to her right, she saw little more than a blur of motion and white cloth.

She spun with a scream of rage.

A heavy blow slammed the back of her head, sending the night into a spin. She fell to her knees on the frosty ground, scrambling for her wits and her gun as she realized there was more than one set of footfalls nearby. She opened her mouth, not to call for help, but to warn Jacob that there were two men, not one.

A hand clamped across her mouth with the strength of a warrior. In the darkness, she could only fight by feel, swinging and kicking, and hitting nothing as he dragged her off the ground by one arm, nearly pinning her inside Jacob's overlarge jacket.

Fear ran a distant second to rage. These men, these *bastards* had taken Hope, Becky and Tiff. They knew where Cooper's family was being held. *They knew.*

Isabella clawed beneath Jacob's heavy jacket and grabbed for her gun.

It wasn't there.

In an instant she remembered Jacob taking it from her, remembered the hot brush of his fingers against her lower back. Then she heard the rasp of metal on metal as her captor pulled a knife.

Panic clawed hard at her throat and she lunged away, knowing she was no use to Cooper's family if she was dead. Her captor growled and grabbed for her. She felt his fist catch in Jacob's jacket, felt the leather bind her arms and shoulders, felt the faint shift in the man's balance as he brought the knife to bear—

And Jacob leaped into the fray with a roar.

He slammed into her captor, driving all three of them to the icy ground in a tangle. Darkness and dizziness confused Isabella. She ripped free of the heavy jacket and scrambled away from the men, who struggled in a silence punctuated by grunts and growled curses, some in Jacob's voice, others low and guttural.

"He's got a knife!" she called, both to warn him and let him know she was away from the struggle, that it was safe for him to shoot her assailant.

Assailant, she realized with a start. Singular.

Where had the other man gone?

Or had she only imagined him?

She lurched to her feet and grabbed for her temples when blood spun in her head from the insult of two concussions in one day. A footstep crackled off to her left, or maybe it was the wind. She followed, trusting Jacob to handle the first man while she tracked the second to his destination.

Maybe even to where Hope and the girls were being held.

That thought blotted out everything else in Isabella's mind. She sucked in a breath and stumbled in the direction of the intermittent footfalls. If she found Cooper's family on her own, rescued them before they were harmed...

Redemption. Maybe even acceptance.

The trees were blacker shapes amid the black night. Her footsteps sounded loud in her head as she strained to hear her quarry. Nothing. Then, up to the right, she heard the unmistakable sound of a car door. He was getting away!

She bolted toward the sound, tripped on a root and went down on her hands and knees. Heart pounding, she scrambled up as an engine fired to life and brake lights flashed cherry-red through the scrub.

No! He couldn't escape—she needed to follow him, to find her protectees!

She burst from the scrub and found herself in an open, sandy strip beside a pitch-black road. The car was a dark, boxy silhouette rolling toward the blacktop. She flung herself in pursuit and the driver, nothing more than a black shadow against the faint gleam of dials, hit the gas. The car roared onto the road and skidded, and the brake lights flashed briefly, gleaming partway off a blacked-out license plate.

Then the car accelerated and was gone.

Heart pounding, stomach fisted on fear and failure, Isabella took two running steps after the man, then stopped. With no gun, no car, she had no way of stopping him.

She leaned her hands on her knees and gasped for breath, for consciousness against the encroaching dizziness.

And heard a noise in the woods behind her. A footstep, stealthy and quiet.

Images of Jacob injured—or worse—jammed her mind and sent her heart into her throat.

She brought her fists up in a fighting stance that felt pitifully inadequate as she stood alone beside the dark road. Hand-to-hand was a poor defense against knives, or a gun.

A shadow moved out of the deeper shadows, barely visible to her night-adapted eyes. A dark figure came at her in a rush and was inside her defenses in an instant.

He grabbed her and shook her. Hard. "Damn it, Isabella. What were you thinking?"

"Jacob." The word burst out of her in a rush, shock tangling with confusion and a sharp flare of desire that didn't seem as inappropriate as it should. "Did you let the other guy get away? What happened?"

Maybe a shaft of moonlight broke through the clouds, or her eyes had fully adapted to the pitch night. Or perhaps she was attuned to the man who suddenly loomed over her. Either way, she saw his eyes flash with anger. "What happened?" The words started on a growl and climbed from there, both in pitch and volume. *"What happened?"*

He tightened his fingers on her arms, making her acutely aware that she'd lost his jacket. The cold cut through her shirt, numbing except for the places where he touched her and heat flared.

He leaned down until they were nearly nose-to-nose.

When he spoke, his voice was low and husky with anger. "By the time I got him down, you were gone. I didn't know whether you'd chased the other guy or been dragged off. I figured you'd been taken, because I couldn't believe you'd be *asinine* enough—" he lifted her nearly to her tiptoes to punctuate the word "—to chase someone unarmed."

"It wasn't my fault I was unarmed," she fired back. "You took my gun." But the words seemed hollow and unimportant, mere sounds on the air between them, which suddenly thickened with sly, shifting warmth. She leaned away from him, feeling trapped when he didn't let go, feeling the need to defend her strength when he didn't ease up. "Besides, I'm a trained agent. I can take care of myself."

"And did your training include basic concepts like never leaving your partner behind?"

His face was too close, his body too well aligned with hers, his presence too solid, too easy to lean into.

She set her chin. "We're not partners."

She could barely see the gleam of his eyes in the heavy darkness, but she felt an unfamiliar jolt of awareness shiver through her body, thought she felt an answering shiver in his. She half expected him to back off, to step away from the anger that sparked between them.

In college, Jacob had been known equally well for the quickness of his temper and his laughter. The man she'd seen since arriving at the Big Sky Bounty Hunters' headquarters was quick with neither of those things. He was tightly guarded. Ruthlessly even-keeled. In control.

But he surprised her by leaning in. He lifted a hand and settled it impersonally at the base of her throat, where she knew he could feel the mad racket of her heart.

He'd think it was from the chase, she told herself, he'd never know her body had kicked into overdrive at his nearness.

Heck, *she* didn't even want to know it.

"No," he said quietly, the words barely ruffling her bangs, "we're not partners. But I didn't know whether you'd followed him or he'd taken you." His fingers tightened slightly on her throat in a flicker of anger, or maybe possessiveness. "I was worried."

The three simple words, which seemed ripped from his gut, slapped straight through her defenses. When was the last time someone had worried, really *worried* about her? It certainly hadn't been during her years at the field office, where she had the reputation of being cold and competent, or during training, where she hadn't bothered returning the other trainees' overtures, knowing that they'd all be separated by their assignments soon enough. And though her mother had certainly worried about her daughter until the day she died, that worry had been smothering, inconsistent, here today, gone the next. No, if Isabella were to look for the last time someone had truly cared enough to worry for her, she'd have to look toward…

Senior year in college, a sneaky voice said at the back of her mind, reminding her of everything that had happened back then, and everything that hadn't. It had been Jacob who had, very briefly, worried for her. Cared about her. Loved her.

Or so she'd thought. But that, like her mother's brief periods of calm, had been nothing more than an illusion. Grief hammered at Isabella's head like pain, in time with the pulse of her heart at the base of her throat where his fingers rested, bringing warmth, bringing memories. Anger surged, muddied with embarrassment that she'd gone back there so quickly, so completely, if only for an instant. She wanted to back away, a mad part of her fearing that he could read inside her and know what she was thinking, what she was feeling, how completely his words and nearness had undone her.

Instead she held her ground, dredged deep and forced professional coolness into her voice when she said, "I didn't come to Big Sky so you could fuss over me, Jacob. I came because your bounty took my protectees. You told your boss you could handle working with me. If you can't…"

She trailed off, letting the implication dangle. *If you can't handle working with me, I'll go someplace else.*

Except there wasn't anyone else she could turn to. She'd be well and truly alone. But would that really be any worse that working with Jacob?

He cursed, dropped his hand from her neck and stepped back, farther into the darkness. "Don't tell me what I can and can't handle. And don't you dare question my professionalism."

She hadn't, which left her wondering whether he was questioning it himself.

The air between then shivered with chill and emotion, an uncertain combination that left her feeling unstable and hating it. She hated that she'd been forced to ask him for help, hated that she'd failed her protectees and allowed Hope and the girls to be taken.

Hated most of all that she felt unstable, teetering between heat and anger, between relief that the bounty hunters were helping her and resentment that she needed their help.

Unstable. Just like her mother had been.

Banishing that thought, she lifted her chin and fisted her hands at her sides. He might not be able to see the defiant gestures, but they helped settle her. Center her. She said, "If you're such a professional, then where is the guy you were fighting with? We'll need to question him."

She thought he muttered something, but when he answered, his voice was calm, nearly blank with its lack of inflection. "He's back in the woods. I knocked him out and strapped him to a tree with his belt and mine before I came after you."

"Oh. Good thinking." Isabella's mouth dried to dust as a completely unnecessary, unwanted memory flared to life in her brain, a Technicolor image of a younger Jacob sliding his belt free of his jeans, looping it around her wrists, and pulling it tight over the metal frame of the bed in her off-campus rental.

She didn't allow herself to follow the sensory image further, but her body remembered, and she cursed the rush of warm wetness that pulsed through her even as she turned away and marched back toward the woods.

It was all an illusion, she reminded herself. What she'd thought of as love had been nothing more than sex.

When Jacob didn't follow, she turned back and

squinted to make out his large shadow against the lighter gleam of the road. "Come on. Let's see what this bastard knows."

He stared at her for a moment, then finally nodded, passed her without a word and led the way back to the scene of the fight.

Isabella followed him through featureless woods, glad for the gleam of moonlight that sliced through the cloud cover and provided a welcome sliver of light. *Please let this guy know where Cooper's family has been taken.* The words beat in her head like a mantra, in time to her uneven footfalls and the growing pulse of a headache. *Please let him tell us.*

Then Jacob halted ahead of her. His shoulders went stiff. And a low, vicious oath filtered back to her on the night air.

She knew it even before she rushed forward to see.

Their captive was gone.

DAMN IT. How could he have been so stupid?

Jacob cursed himself as he drove out to the copper mining area, going too fast and purposely hitting every bump. The Jeep slewed and swerved and rattled him nearly hard enough to chase away the reality of what had happened at the Golf Resort.

He'd messed up, that was what had happened. He'd had the bastard and lost him because he'd lost his focus. He'd been so worried about Isabella—a trained operative—that he'd done a crummy job securing his captive, and they'd wound up with nothing more than a generic leather belt crumpled at the base of a pine tree.

Which left them with nothing. No captive. No new leads. Not even clear proof that Boone and his men were involved. The more he thought about it, the more it seemed like the letters written on Secretary Cooper's chest could be a false lead. The MMFAFA had never worked internationally before. Why start now?

People didn't change that drastically over time.

He gritted his teeth and gripped the steering wheel harder when the Jeep slid to the side of the overgrown track. Once a main road to the copper mines high on a mountainside, the trail was now little more than a fire access road, and a poor one at that. With the late dawn just beginning to stain the sky red, and the trees closed in around him, Jacob had to rely on the bouncing headlight beams and focus on his driving.

Which was a relief, as it deflected his mind away from other things, such as the men who'd been watching them search the chalet, and the near-crazy fear he'd felt when he'd realized Isabella was gone. The blinding anger that had flared when he'd seen she was safe.

His foot pressed down on the gas and the Jeep leaped forward, nearly slewing off the road. He corrected with a curse, but didn't let up, instead driving faster, halfway thinking he could outrun the burn of anger in his gut, the flare of heat everywhere else.

He hadn't managed it by the time he parked among the pickup trucks the other bounty hunters had driven. Instead he shoved the too intense emotions aside, locked them away so he could deal with them—and their auburn-haired source—later.

Or not.

He found the others outside the first mine, waiting for him in front of a barred gate they'd clearly picked and relocked. Tony and Mike had called in four others to help search for the source of the green-tinted dirt. Jacob was startled to see Big Sky's leader among them.

Then again, by history and right, Boone Fowler was Cameron's bounty. His prize. And anything that got them closer to capturing the MMFAFA fugitives brought them closer to Cameron's final reckoning with Fowler.

Jacob nodded at the others. "Find anything?"

"Nothing obvious." Tony gestured with the fifty-pound rucksack he held over his shoulder as though it weighed five. "We've taken samples for comparison." Then he narrowed his eyes at Jacob's face. "What happened to you?"

Jacob shoved his hands in his pockets. "Two men were watching Cooper's chalet."

There were no exclamations of shock or disbelief from the other hunters. Instead they went silent. Still. Intense. Then Cameron ordered, "Tell us."

Jacob sketched the incident, including all the details he could remember. He didn't gloss over the part where he'd had one of the guys and lost him, but he omitted the roaring fear that had dogged him through the woods on Isabella's trail and how it scared him to the bone to think she might actually have *caught* the other guy, and what then?

Abduction.

If she was lucky.

With an almost physical effort, he pulled his thoughts

back on track. "The guys—well, at least the one I fought with—had night-vision goggles. I have to guess they pulled them on once I doused the lights in the chalet. It sure gave them a heck of an advantage."

"Night vision!" Cameron said thoughtfully. "How did Boone get his hands on technology like that only a few weeks out of The Fortress?"

Dull surprise rattled through Jacob when he realized he'd never even considered the question. He'd been too caught up in Isabella, in the confusion. It was proof positive that they weren't good for each other.

Correction—it was proof positive that he couldn't handle seeing her. So far she'd been nothing but professional, which galled him on a too personal level.

"The MMFAFA is a tight-knit group," Mike offered. "Maybe he's called some of his old contacts." The body language expert glanced over at Jacob, who stiffened, awaiting a comment about him running to Isabella's rescue. But Mike merely continued. "Besides, you can buy just about anything on the Internet these days."

"Not like these you can't. They were state-of-the-art." Jacob shifted from foot to foot, wanting to move rather than stand around talking while the clock ran down on their bounty. On the abductees.

"But you said yourself it was dark." Cameron shrugged. "They could've been mail order."

"Or they could've come from Lunkinburg," Jacob snapped. His fingers tapped a complicated rhythm against his leg. "For all we know, the letters on Cooper's chest meant something else, or were planted to throw suspicion onto Boone's people. This could have absolutely nothing to do with our bounty."

"It could have everything to do with them." Cameron's eyes went flat, the way they did when he was mad and trying not to show it. "And what does it really matter? Secretary Cooper's family is missing and Agent Gray has asked us to help. So what's your point?"

Anger tangled with resentment and Jacob felt suddenly crowded. He cracked his knuckles and walked away, then back. Then he shrugged and shot his boss a look. "Hell. I don't know what my point is anymore."

Cam's eyes softened a hint, though he turned away so the others couldn't see. "Yeah. I figured as much." His gesture sent the others to their vehicles, leaving him and Jacob alone on the rocky incline. "How is she?"

"Isabella?" Jacob asked, more to buy himself time than because there was any question who Cam meant. "She's okay. She's tough." More than tough, she was dedicated and professional, and he wasn't sure why that ticked him off so badly. "I left her back at the headquarters and told her she could crash in your guest room. I hope that was okay."

Cam and his wife Mia lived in the big, rustic cabin with their daughter and the housekeeper, Trudy, so there was always someone minding the headquarters—and the expensive high-tech gadgetry on the lower levels.

The other hunters all rented or owned homes down the mountain, in town. Jacob had briefly thought about bringing Isabella back to his place, but it hadn't felt right, so he'd taken her to the cabin.

"Of course that's okay. Trudy can look after her," Cam said as though Isabella needed looking after.

The very idea would probably make her furious, Jacob thought, but the sentiment didn't bring a grin. Instead it made him feel worse, as though he should have stayed.

God, he was a mess.

"Come on." Cam jerked his head toward the vehicles. "Tony says there are a half dozen copper mines for us to check, only two of which have good roads leading in. If we don't find anything conclusive, it could be a long day."

"On the heels of a long night," Jacob agreed. But as he followed Cam to his truck, figuring they could pick up the Jeep later, Jacob found himself partway hoping it would be a long day.

The more tired he was, the less Isabella would get to him.

He hoped.

EXHAUSTED, frustrated and hosting the headache that just wouldn't quit, Isabella tried not to snap when there was yet another knock at the guest room door. She pinched the bridge of her nose. "Yes?"

The door opened and the Big Sky housekeeper entered, bearing a small tray. "I brought you some soup and tea."

Isabella didn't bother reminding Trudy that she'd already said she wasn't hungry. The silver-haired housekeeper had proven a formidable opponent, taking zero heed of Isabella's wish to be left alone. Trudy had bullied her into the shower, stolen her clothes and replaced them with borrowed sweats in a soft peach color, no doubt the property of the dark-haired woman in the photographs adorning the far wing of the cabin, where the boss and his family lived.

When Isabella had gone looking for a phone, she'd been neatly rerouted to her room. Now she was being fed, whether she liked it or not.

The worst part was that she actually felt a little better than she had when she arrived, fresh on the heels of a long, silent drive with Jacob.

Aware that Trudy stood, looking down at her with an expectant expression underlain with a hint of steel, Isabella sighed and gestured at the small desk beside the pin-neat bed. "Fine. I'll eat."

"You'll eat in bed," the housekeeper corrected, setting the tray on a narrow lap desk. She shooed Isabella between the sheets.

"Bossy, aren't you?" But Isabella stretched out. Then she tried not to groan as the soft mattress cupped her tired, aching bones.

"Only with those who deserve it," Trudy replied, but her hands were gentle when she settled the tray across Isabella's lap and set a cordless phone, notebook and pen within easy reach. "Now eat. If you're still awake when you're done, you can make those calls."

If Isabella hadn't been so tired and beat up, she might have resented Trudy's coddling. But at that moment she found the woman soothing. Comforting.

So she forced a smirk. "And what if I'm asleep? Will you tuck me in?"

"If you like." Trudy headed for the door, so Isabella couldn't see the woman's expression, but the set of her shoulders spoke of amusement rather than ire, and the bump beneath her sweatshirt warned that she carried a gun at the small of her back.

The sight shouldn't have been as reassuring as it was.

The door closed behind Trudy and Isabella glanced at the phone, notebook and pen. She had calls to make. She had few friends within the Service, but one or two people owed her favors, and she wasn't above collecting. Even better, at least one of the people she had in mind wasn't jacked into the gossip mill—he might not yet know she'd failed her protectees and been suspended.

Pending a psych eval.

The thoughts soured her already uncertain stomach. What if everyone already knew she'd been suspended? What if they all believed she'd cracked?

"Let them believe what they want," she said out loud. "It's not important."

But instead of reaching for the phone, she reached for the food Trudy had left for her.

She'd eat first, then make the calls.

"ANYTHING?" JACOB ASKED a grungy Tony as the other man emerged from the depths of yet another green-tainted, half-unsteady mineshaft. The geologist still carried the heavy sample knapsack as though it weighed nothing, even though it now contained samples from various spots within four abandoned mines.

"Nothing." Tony grunted. Six hours into their search,

nearing high noon after a sleepless night, they had lapsed into monosyllables and single word answers.

Without speaking, the bounty hunters—down to Jacob, Tony, Mike and Cameron, the others having left for other tasks—climbed into the truck and headed for the fifth mine.

They'd left this one and one other until last, because the access roads were nearly impassable. In fact, the old road was so bad they were forced to park their vehicle near a washout and hike the last half mile, which did nothing to help Jacob's temper.

The mine, when they reached it, proved to be the shabbiest-looking of the bunch. It wasn't gated or locked as the others had been—and were required to be by law—and part of the main opening had fallen in, giving the cavern a lopsided, sneering look. There was no sign of life, no evidence that any human had been here since it had been abandoned decades earlier.

"Another bust," Mike mumbled. The normally cheerful body language expert had gotten progressively more sour as the search wore on.

"Let's check it out anyway." Jacob led the way inside and immediately pulled his jacket closed against the dampness. The cold was natural this time of year and at this elevation, but the moisture seemed strange, even a little warmer than it ought to be. He flipped up his collar. "Yeesh. Weird air."

"Maybe there's a hot spring at the back," Tony suggested, shifting his shoulders to settle the heavy pack more comfortably. "Maybe that's why the mine closed so much earlier than the others."

Cameron frowned. "And maybe that accounts for the smell."

But the fine buzz that ran through Jacob told him that the tendril of that sickly scent didn't come from any hot spring.

It was the smell of death.

Chapter Five

"Damn it, woman, I said, *Get me another ice pack!*"
Lyle Nelson's voice carried into the mobile home,
where Hope sat with her daughters, trying to keep them
quiet, trying not to let them know she was afraid.
Through the greasy front window, she saw her whip-
thin, brown-haired captor prop himself higher in his
lawn chair and crane his neck to see where she'd gone.

She stood and leaned down to place a kiss on each
of the girls's cheeks. "Stay here a moment. Mommy
will be right back."

Their answering silence deafened her, tightened the
ball of dread in her stomach. They were too quiet. Too
still. Too pliant. In the day since they'd been taken from
the chalet, shoved into a dark SUV and driven to this
godforsaken place high in the hills, the girls had slipped
into a trancelike state, barely responding to anything she
said or did.

Just now, they clung to each other, their only movement the track of their identical blue eyes as she walked
two steps into the kitchen area, grabbed a clinic-brand

instant ice pack and smashed it against the counter to start the cooling chemical reaction.

What was this experience doing to them? she wondered, focusing on the long-term consequences because the short-term questions and answers were too terrifying to consider.

Like the main question: what had they done to Louis?

Was he dead? Alive? What horrors must he be going through? Hope's heart cried for him, because she knew her husband well. So while she knew that Secretary of Defense Cooper would never negotiate with hostage takers, Louis Cooper the man would move heaven and earth to save his wife and family.

If he was able to.

The thought brought gut-wrenching tears, and she turned away from the girls on the pretext of rummaging in one of the cheap cabinets, though she'd already determined there was nothing in the kitchen she could use as a weapon.

Lyle's voice cracked from outside. "You bring it here now, or I'll take those babies of yours and I'll—"

She was out the door before he could finish the sentence. "Here's your ice."

The bastard's thin lips curved in victory and he gestured with the shotgun he held across his lap. "Put it on my leg. Gently."

She did as she was told, overcoming the urge to jam the pack down on the half-doctored bullet wound he must have gotten during the kidnapping, and press until he howled.

But Lyle had the gun, and he was in charge, at least

until Boone Fowler returned. The militia leader had left hours earlier and put his second lieutenant in charge of the prisoners, with Kane Myers and Ray Fleming standing by as backup.

It terrified her that she knew each of their names. Fowler had introduced them all one by one, staring at her with cold, black eyes and a sneer on his scarred face. The action had meant one of two things. Either they wanted credit for the kidnapping or they weren't planning to let her live to testify against them.

The very thought had her pressing down on the ice pack.

Lyle shouted a curse. He leaped to his feet and the ice pack fell to the floor when he grabbed Hope by her throat.

His fingers bit into her flesh. He dropped the shotgun with a clatter, pulled a semiautomatic pistol from his belt and held it against her temple.

"I could do it, you know." He stroked the gun muzzle along her cheek, pressing harder onto the bruises until she shifted with a whimper. "I could kill you and tell Boone you tried to run. Then I'd be all alone to look after those pretty girls of yours. Your husband would never know the difference. Never know what happened." He pressed closer and lowered his voice to a lover's purr. "I could do it."

No! Dread spiraled through her, mixed with desperation. Her knees threatened to buckle at the feel of the gun muzzle on her face, the sweaty, blood-tinged smell of the man who held her. She opened her mouth to deny him, to beg, but before the plea could form, the trailer door banged open with a sound like a gunshot.

Lyle spun her around, clamped an arm across her throat and leveled the pistol at the sound. "Freeze or you're a dead man!"

Kane Meyers, a bull of a man sporting gray-shot hair and a grizzled beard though he looked shy of forty, froze. Then he chuckled—a dry, scratchy sound. "Chill, dude, it's only me and Ray."

Lyle lowered the weapon and growled, "Don't sneak up on a guy like that. You're liable to get yourself dead." He shoved Hope toward the trailer. "Get in the back. And keep those babies quiet, or else."

The threat hardly seemed necessary, but Hope turned and bolted into the trailer, wanting to be away from Lyle and his guns. Once inside, she banged the door shut, checked on the girls—still wide-eyed and too silent— and held a finger to her lips.

Then she crept back and put her ear to the breezy gap in the sagging door.

Lyle's rough voice came first. "What did you see over at the resort?"

"You were right," Kane's voice answered, "the bitch that shot you came back. She had three guys with her, and some equipment. They stayed in the place for an hour, maybe more, then left."

Isabella! Hope thought with a flash of excitement.

She angled her face against the crack and peeked through. Lyle had his back to her, but she could see the other men's faces. Kane seemed fine, but Ray's lower lip was split nearly down to his chin, his clothes torn, his belt missing.

Lyle leaned down, retrieved the shotgun and leaned on it like a crutch. "What aren't you telling me?"

The men exchanged a glance before Kane lowered his voice and said, "She heard us, or maybe the guy with her did. They chased us for a bit, but we got away. I took the car and circled back for Ray. No worries."

Lyle cursed. "Did they make you? And who were the men? Cops? Damn it, we told Cooper no cops!"

Hope stifled a gasp of joy. Louis was alive!

"No, not cops. They weren't G-men. They were more like mercs," Ray said, his higher-pitched voice scratching along Hope's nerve endings like steel wool as she grappled with the information. No cops. So what was Isabella doing there? And who was she with?

More importantly, where was Louis? Isabella never would have left her protectee unless he was hurt.

Or worse.

He's alive, Hope told herself. *He's fine.*

But deep down inside, she wasn't sure she believed it. If he was fine, why hadn't he been with Isabella? Why wasn't he tearing through the chalet, looking for clues as to where the men had taken her?

Why wasn't he looking for her?

"Must've been one of those bounty hunters." Lyle spat on the ground near Kane's booted feet. "Damn. If they saw you…"

His anger gave her hope. The trailer was smack in the middle of nowhere—thus the crushable insta-ice packs rather than the real thing. They had reached it via an overgrown access road that probably wasn't even on any map, but it hadn't been more than a half hour drive from the Golf Resort.

Those bounty hunters might be close. They might even have followed Kane and Ray from the resort.

Lyle cursed. "We're going to need to move the woman and the brats."

"You're right," a new voice said, startling Hope and sending a bolt of fear through her chest.

Boone Fowler had arrived.

And if Lyle, with his guns and his too close interest in the little girls scared her, Boone, with his scarred face and dead black eyes, downright terrified her.

Boone stepped into her view and glanced at the trailer as though he'd heard her thoughts, as though he knew she was listening at the crack.

"We're moving," he said in a voice that brooked no argument. "I've sent the others ahead to secure our new home. We'll travel in twos and threes to deflect attention." He handed Lyle a thick envelope. "Your new name and info is in here. You take one of the girls and give the other to Kane. I've got some knockout drops that should keep them quiet for you."

"No! You leave my babies alone!" Without thought, without conscious decision, Hope burst from the trailer and flew at Boone, fingers curled into talons.

He caught her and twisted her arm up high behind her back. Pain slashed through her body and she screamed.

The sound was echoed from inside the trailer, then broke to rising wails from first one twin, then the other.

Boone twisted her arm higher. Her vision grayed and she slumped against him, hating the feel of his lean, too hot body against hers. His voice sounded unaffected when he said, "I'll take the woman and see that she behaves."

Lyle nodded, pocketed the tickets and fake IDs, then jerked his head in the direction of the Golf Resort. "And the Secret Service bitch and the others? What about them?"

Boone shrugged and said with dead finality in his voice, "Don't worry. They'll be taken care of."

Now it was Hope's turn to cry.

OUT AT THE copper mines, Isabella found the bounty hunters' vehicles without trouble, but only because Cameron had drawn her a map when she'd turned down his offer of an escort. He probably would have insisted, but with two of his men off checking the robbed clinic for evidence, and several others gone who only knew where, he'd been out of manpower.

Which was just fine with her. She didn't need a babysitter.

A sense of watching eyes prickled the back of her neck as she walked the rubbled half mile to the abandoned mine, but after pausing to check her laces and surreptitiously scan the woods on either side of the washed-out road for the third time, she decided that any onlookers were of the four-legged, furry variety.

Still, she was reassured by the press of her weapon at the small of her back.

She paused at the mouth of the mine and looked back the way she'd come, but there was no motion. No sound. Just the feeling of watching eyes.

She shrugged and ducked inside.

The dank air was a fetid slap, but she ignored it and followed the sound of masculine voices. She immediately picked out Jacob's low, carefully controlled tones and cursed herself for the instant flush of awareness.

He was a means to an end, nothing more. She needed his help, his resources. More importantly, Hope and the girls needed all the help they could get. She couldn't let personal feelings muddy that simple fact.

She had a job to do, damn it.

She took a dozen more steps into the cavern and her heart stopped at the smell of death.

Hope! Becky! Tiff!

Failure and fear were a double blow. Isabella swallowed the scream that threatened to press between her teeth and bolted toward the voices.

She rounded a jagged rock outcropping and plunged into darkness, then back into light filtering from a collapsed spot high ahead.

She saw the body.

And was grabbed from behind. A heavy arm clamped across her collarbones and her arm was neatly twisted behind her back. *Caught!*

She screeched and tried to twist away, nearly breaking her own arm in the process.

Jacob's voice cursed and she was suddenly free.

She ignored the fine buzz running through her body at the rough touch of his hands. She spun and glared at him. "You could have just said hello."

"Yeah," he returned, "and you could have been Fowler or one of his men."

She ignored him to stare down at the sad pile of human remains half propped against the cavern's rock wall.

The sad pile of *male* human remains.

Her first emotion was blessed relief that it wasn't Hope or one of the girls. Her second emotion was dull horror.

The poor bastard had been shot neatly between the eyes, close enough to leave muzzle flash on the gray skin of his forehead.

He'd been executed.

Jacob shifted as though to put himself between her and the body. "You recognize him?"

She shook her head, vaguely aware of the two other bounty hunters, Mike and Tony, standing in the shadows, watching the exchange. "No. Should I?"

He nodded. "Yeah. He's one of Boone Fowler's men. One of the escaped fugitives. Derek Horton."

The body looked sunk in on itself in death. In Isabella's mind, the corpse went instantly from *poor bastard* to simply *bastard* with the knowledge that Horton had helped kidnap Cooper's family.

Or had he?

Moving no further into the shallow rock alcove—lest she disturb evidence the police would later process—she squatted on her heels and stared at the body, training clicking into gear when nothing else seemed to make sense. She sniffed. "He stinks."

"Yeah," Jacob said from his position nearer the main cavern, "he's probably been here for a couple of days. Corpses don't ripen quickly 'round here in the winter."

She wondered whether he was trying to frighten her or whether he was simply stating a fact.

"Maybe less," Tony countered. The geologist glanced around the cavern. "The air is…weird in here. Too warm. That could speed up decomposition more than we'd expect. I'd like to have a look farther into the mine to see if I can find the hot spring or whatever is generating the heat."

"No." Jacob's response was curt, his expression grim. "We head back down the mountain and call the cops. I don't want any hint of an evidence problem when we get the bounty back in custody and they're pulled up on the new murder charges."

There was a moment of silence before the other hunters nodded, a tense undercurrent that Isabella didn't understand, wasn't sure she wanted to. The bounty hunters were a tight-knit group of men who knew each other well. She didn't do tight knit and she didn't care to be known.

"Let's go," Mike said, jerking his chin toward the mine entrance. "We can call the cops from headquarters and claim the bounty while we're at it." His lips tipped upward in a wry grimace. "We get paid dead or alive—this time we'll collect on *dead*."

But as they emerged from the alcove into the main cavern, Isabella sensed their frustration. She hung back and let Mike and Tony move on ahead, then said quietly to Jacob, "There weren't any other leads?"

He glanced at her impatiently, as though he was in a hurry to get to headquarters, or maybe to get away from her. "Signs of a campfire and a couple of latrine pits.

Some garbage, most of it older. The crime scene people will have to tell us what it all means."

But she'd already seen the bounty hunters process Cooper's chalet and knew darn well they didn't need to wait for any crime scene report. Ergo, they already knew there was nothing to find beyond a corpse and more questions.

"Why did you come out here?" he asked abruptly.

Because I needed your help, she almost answered before she realized that he was asking why she'd come to the mine, not why she'd come to him in the first place.

She clenched her teeth against the old insecurities and told herself to get a grip. "Because I made some calls." Once she'd woken from five badly needed hours of sleep. "Secretary Cooper is back in Washington, and the story is already breaking."

"He's told the media about the kidnapping?" Jacob asked quickly.

"No." She shook her head. "He's reversed his position on sending troops into Lunkinburg. Now he says we should wait and try more diplomatic approaches."

"Whoa. Wait." Jacob stopped dead near the mouth of the cave, where the other hunters waited. He dragged a hand through his hair and looked, for a frozen instant in time, like the younger man she remembered, angry and a little confused.

Like the man she'd fallen in love with.

Isabella swallowed hard and jammed her fists into the pockets of her jeans. She felt the bulge of her gun at her waistband and used the sensation to drive the memories away.

That naive girl had wanted a home and family, not guns and action. She'd changed. Jacob had changed.

There was no going back, and she was smart enough not to want to go forward. If they had been headed in different directions during college, they were even further apart in their goals now. She wanted to do her duty, to be the best and to move up within the Service. Jacob...he hunted men for money.

She was a patriot. He was a mercenary.

Even as the thought formed, she felt faintly ashamed, as though the word couldn't possibly encompass the man beside her. But before she could reconsider the definition, Mike waved from the cave entrance.

"Hey," he called. "You two coming?"

"In a minute. We've got some new info." When the others came back inside the cave, Jacob briefly repeated what she'd told him about Cooper's flip-flop on the Lunkinburg issue, finishing with, "But that makes no sense. The letters written on his chest suggest that Boone and his militia are the kidnappers. Derek Horton's corpse proves it. The dirt in the chalet had to have come from this mine, and Horton's body was waiting for us, almost as though..."

He trailed off and Isabella saw the wrinkle just as he did. "Almost as though it was planted," she finished quietly.

"Yeah." He glanced at her, then looked toward the trees outside as though searching for the same watcher she'd sensed earlier.

"So what do we do now?" Tony asked.

Jacob paused, then said almost unwillingly, "We split

up." He shot a glance back into the mine, then out toward the trees. "I want you two to stay here and wait for Murphy and the cops. Isabella and I will go down and call them now."

His actions told her that he felt it, too. The sense of being watched from all directions.

"Then what?" The question came from the other man, Mike, who watched Jacob with an intensity Isabella found unnerving, as though there was an entirely separate conversation being held on a nonverbal level, one that she wasn't privy to.

"Then we chase the leads." Jacob shoved his hands into his pockets. "We'll need to follow up on the clinic robbery, and I'm going to ask the boss to have Blackhaw bring in the dogs. It's a long shot that they'll be able to track anything beyond the road, but if anyone can coax them onto a scent, it'll be Trevor." The half-Cherokee ex-commando had a way with Big Sky's animal partners. Jacob continued. "And we'll want to look into everyone at the Golf Resort. They got in through Isabella's motion detectors and security, which means they're either *very* good or they had inside help." He glanced at her almost in apology. "I'm betting the latter."

"I'm ahead of you on that," she said evenly, feeling the sting of stupidity, of mistakes made, of time passing. "I went back through my files, and two individuals in and near Cooper's chalet have tenuous ties to the MMFAFA. One is a young cop on the security detail. His sister's husband is a gun dealer who was questioned about selling to Boone Fowler without proper docu-

mentation. The case was dropped." And now it pre-
sented them a hell of a challenge. How could they question a cop about an abduction nobody official knew
about? "And the other is a maid. Six or seven years ago,
she was picked up with her boyfriend when a speeding
stop turned into a shootout. The boyfriend was MM-
FAFA. He got three-to-five and she's been clean since."

Jacob scowled. "And you didn't think these were
problems when you ran your background checks? Did
it escape your attention that the MMFAFA is a priority
around here right now, what with Boone and his men
escaping from jail and *killing* the governor?"

Frustration raked at Isabella with greedy claws.
"Don't tell me how to do my job!" She rounded on him
and cranked her volume, more because she was angry
with herself than with him. "Of *course* I was aware of
the situation. But I was assigned to protect Secretary
Cooper from the person or persons who had been sending him threatening letters about Lunkinburg, which has
nothing to do with your fugitives!"

Or so she'd thought. Now they had conflicting evidence, in the form of bloody letters and Horton's corpse,
pointing toward the MMFAFA, and the threatening letters and Cooper's abrupt shift in policy, which aimed
them back toward the Lunkinburg sympathizers.

But she hadn't known. She couldn't have known.
And she'd been alone in her assignment, so she'd had
to vet her contacts as thoroughly as possible and then
make a judgment call.

Guilt scratched with the knowledge that she'd called
it wrong.

After a long moment Jacob looked away. "What's done is done. Let's just fix it."

His silent condemnation sliced deep and left her bleeding, but she lifted her chin. "I have a plan."

"So do I," he countered. He jerked his head toward the mine. "Mike and Tony will wait for the cops. Once you and I have made the calls that need to be made, we'll head for Washington. I think it's time to pay Cooper a little visit and find out what's really going on."

She wanted to curse at him, to swipe at him, to do something that would spark a fight and relieve the awful guilt, remove the memory of the smell of death.

Instead she crossed her arms. "I already snagged us tickets for first thing tomorrow morning." *So there,* she thought, though she knew it shouldn't feel like a competition between them when they were supposed to be working together.

He met her eyes for an instant and she read something unexpected in them. Regret, perhaps, or apology, neither of which she deserved. But his voice held no hint of either when he said, "Fine. Washington it is. But Big Sky has its own jet and I prefer to fly myself."

JACOB, ISABELLA and another of the bounty hunters, Joseph Brown, arrived at the local airport early the next morning, only to find that the jet wasn't quite ready for them. Still hungry after missing several meals the day before, Jacob aimed them from the small terminal to the main jetway so they could grab food.

The airport was crowded with an assortment of students coming and going for the new school year, early skiers headed north, and foliage watchers hoping for one last weekend. Or so he guessed from the outfits, which ranged from preppies wearing pressed flannels from trendy faux-lumberjack catalogs to impoverished ski bums hoping for one more season on the slopes.

And what was he hoping for?

A quick resolution to this mess, he thought, glancing at the woman beside him. A quick return to his normal life, which he liked just fine.

As though sensing the direction of his thoughts, she darted a look in his direction, and when the fast-food line next surged forward, she hung back to stand beside Joseph.

The younger bounty hunter—also a former Special Forces operative—was scowling, but that was nothing new. Ever since his three-year-old marriage had gone south for good, Joseph had been in a foul mood. Dark blond and strong as a steel bar, the expert tracker had followed his faithless wife halfway across the country for an explanation.

He'd returned a changed man. Quiet. Morose. Even angry. And though he'd eased up some over the six months since, he didn't smile when Isabella said something to him, too softly for Jacob to hear.

Joseph merely frowned harder and shook his head.

"Sir?" a voice intruded, snapping Jacob from his too intense concentration on the man and woman at his back. "What can I get you?"

Jacob yanked his attention to the menu and ordered at random. Once they all had their greasy paper bags in hand, he gestured toward a bank of seats near one of the domestic gates. The digital crawl above the door advertised a flight leaving for Sacramento in under an hour. "Keep your eyes open," he warned. "We're not on vacation here."

"Didn't think we were," Joseph snapped. He glared at Jacob, claimed a seat and crossed his arms over his wide chest. "I'll keep my eyes open from here."

Jacob scowled, annoyed with himself, with the situation. He glanced over at Isabella, at her heart-shaped face, auburn hair and take-no-prisoners, mossy-green eyes, and felt a tender, protective quiver run through his body.

Not good.

He cursed and pushed himself to his feet, needing to walk. But she was a step ahead of him, already moving across the nearby waiting area. She crouched beside a dark-haired, clean-shaven man holding a sleeping child.

Her eyes were haunted.

Caution prickled along the back of Jacob's neck and he strode to join her, nearing them in time to hear her say, "Your son is beautiful. What's his name?"

"Malachai," the man replied quietly, so as not to wake the boy.

Jacob shrugged off the quick tightness in his shoulders and turned away, baffled by Isabella's actions, annoyed that the maternal instincts she'd made no secret of years earlier still held power over her. Damn it, he was trying to be a professional, why couldn't she?

She joined him a moment later and glanced up at him. No doubt his face looked as stiff as it felt.

She frowned. "What's the matter with you?"

"Nothing." When her eyes darkened, he cursed himself and relented. He gestured with his chin back toward the waiting area, which now stirred and buzzed with energy as the boarding orders went out over the loudspeaker. "Cute kid."

She shrugged. "Cute enough. He reminded me…" She trailed off, took a breath and squared her shoulders. "He reminded me of Cooper's little girls."

"Oh." Jacob winced at the pain in her voice and the dig of shame. Then suspicion pierced and he spun to glare at the guy. *"Oh!"*

"Don't." She touched his arm. "It's just a single father and his son going to visit family. The security officers at the desk said his papers check out, and the child is drooling on his shoulder, completely at ease. It's nothing." She let out a breath. "Just wishful thinking."

"Hmm." He stared at the man a heartbeat longer, partly to buy himself time to buffer against her touch, and partly to compare the man's face to those of the militiamen he sought.

The "father" was clean-cut where Boone's followers tended toward unkempt beards, and that was part of the problem. A quick swipe with a razor could go a long way toward changing a man's appearance, as could new clothes and a five-dollar box of hair dye.

"You guys all set?" Joseph glanced at his watch and pushed to his feet. "The jet should be ready by now."

"Come on." Isabella tugged at Jacob's arm. "I told you, it's nothing. They're clean."

But something nagged at the hard ball of instinct in

Jacob's gut, the one that had kept him alive through numerous official—and not-so official—airstrike runs in the Special Forces and made him a successful bounty hunter in the years since.

He watched as the man stood with the small child draped bonelessly—was the kid truly asleep or really drugged?—across his shoulder. The guy handed over his boarding pass and glanced around. His eyes caught Jacob's, then slid away. Was that a flash of recognition? Of fear?

Hell, he didn't know, not even when the father and son disappeared down the gangplank. So Jacob stood a moment longer, waiting for the sense of warning to fade. But it didn't. Not even when he followed Isabella and Joseph out to Big Sky's jets.

No, even then the tingle remained, telling him he'd missed something.

Or someone.

FROM HER POSITION in the waiting area of the next nonstop flight to Los Angeles, Hope watched Isabella and the two strangers walk away.

She wanted to stand and scream for them to come back, for them to rescue her.

But she didn't. She couldn't. Her daughters had flown out ahead, with Lyle and Kane, and Boone sat beside her with the men's cell numbers on speed dial, nearly daring her.

Just try it, she could almost hear him think. *Just try calling for help. Your babies will be dead before help arrives. I promise.*

So she stayed quiet and still, and forced her eyes back to the magazine in her lap.

Boone chuckled quietly. "A wise decision."

Then he rummaged in his carry-on and pulled out a second cell phone, different from the one he'd used to call his men. He hit a single button and angled his body away from her.

"Everything is fine," he answered shortly when the call rang through. "The others are en route and my lovely wife and I will board our flight in ten minutes. However, I saw three friends of ours just now. Two boys from Big Sky and Ms. Isabella Gray."

He paused and listened, and Hope saw a dull red flush climb his throat beneath the heavier, glue-on beard he'd used as part of his disguise. After two days in his company, she knew him well enough to know that the color was anger, not embarrassment.

Which made her wonder who was on the other end of the phone. She hadn't thought Boone was the sort to take grief from anyone.

"I don't know where they're going," he answered shortly. "They went down into the private terminal. Small planes, corporate jets, that sort of thing."

His eyes slid to her and locked on. His lips turned up slightly at the corners, twisting the makeup-covered scar tissue into something unseemly. "Good. I'm counting on you to take care of them. We can't afford any interference."

Chapter Six

Once the Big Sky jet was in the air, Joseph folded his arms across his massive chest, closed his eyes and dropped off to sleep.

Isabella had to believe it was genuine. Nobody would fake a snore like that on purpose.

Unfortunately she was too keyed up to sleep, which left her sitting just behind the empty copilot's seat with a perfect profile view of the pilot. Jacob.

She tried not to watch his deft motions at the controls, tried not to strain to catch the sound of his familiar voice issuing unfamiliar call signs and cross checks.

Tried not to think of how sexy it was that he flew like a natural, as if the jet was a powerful extension of his muscled arms and legs.

Heat bloomed in her body and she turned away to focus on the paperback she'd jammed in her carry-on. *Keep to yourself, Isabella,* she told herself. *It's worked this long.*

But a small voice deep inside questioned the mantra. If keeping to herself worked so well, how come she was cut off from the support of the Service? How come it had been so easy for her superiors to give Cooper a nod and a wink and dump her on administrative leave?

Had anyone at the home office fought for her? Had anyone even noticed she was off the active roster?

Depression settled around her like a wet, moldy blanket.

"What's your problem?"

It took a moment for her to realize the question had come from the pilot's seat, not her own mind. When it registered, her hackles rose. "I haven't got a problem. What's yours?"

"No problem. Just making conversation in my own half-assed way." Jacob glanced back at her, then angled his head toward the copilot's seat. "Want to ride up front?"

Why? she almost asked, unsure why he would choose that moment to talk to her when he'd made it darned clear he was avoiding deep discussions up to that point.

Maybe because they were thousands of feet above the ground, or maybe because they were alone save for Joseph's snoring bulk.

So she didn't ask why. Instead she took the copilot's chair and strapped in.

She gazed out at the clouds for a moment in silence, glanced over at him to watch his strong, tanned forearms shift and bunch while he made adjustments she couldn't even feel. His hair seemed more chestnut than brown in the afternoon sunlight above the clouds and his eyes glinted a green counterpoint to the blue sky.

Swallowing, she returned her attention to the world outside, the clouds below them. It was a strange, heady feeling to sit up front like this, she decided, and felt a flash of envy for his skill.

She pitched her voice to carry over the engine noise and through his headset. "You're good at this."

He glanced over, eyes unreadable. "It gives me a sense of control."

At the word, the sentiment, her moment of contentment soured. "Right. Controlling your own life was always big with you." She frowned. "Which is why you joined the army two weeks after we graduated."

She instantly regretted the words and the sarcasm, knowing there was no need for them to go back there, but Jacob didn't seem to mind. It was as though he realized they needed to have this conversation and had picked the time and place.

On his turf. The sky.

"Oh, yeah," he answered. "The army was definitely about controlling my own life." He punched a few buttons on the console, then leaned back and looked at her, green eyes piercing. "I don't remember how much we talked about my parents and what they wanted for me. Conversation wasn't really our thing."

When he left the comment hanging, she nodded reluctantly and tried to keep her face from heating. "True."

Their thing had been sex. Raw, primal, needy sex, the kind that had left her hungry again the moment the off-campus apartment door closed behind him, and had kept her thinking about him every moment they were apart.

Looking back, their brief relationship seemed almost unhealthy. But that many years ago, it had felt like *everything* and it had left her shattered when it was gone.

Luckily, she'd learned her lesson from past mistakes. She could ignore the warm flush shivering through her body at the conjured memories, and she could turn away from the ache that hit square in her chest at the sight of those agile fingers adjusting a lever here, a dial there.

She was a grown-up now. An agent. She carried a gun and had protected the First Lady of the United States. She was far removed from the needy girl who'd once hung on Jacob's arm and begged him to stay.

Though silence had hovered between them, Jacob continued as though the conversation had never paused. "My father is a politician, my mother a politician's wife. I was meant to be the next generation, maybe make a run all the way to the top. They had it all planned out. The poli-sci degree at Georgetown, law school, some tasteful networking…"

He trailed off and Isabella felt a low, angry burn. She thought of her mother, of the drugs and therapy that had been too little, too late. "Poor baby."

A muscle in his jaw jumped and flexed, but he kept his attention fixed on her, his eyes on hers as though he was willing her to understand. "I know it sounds juvenile, and maybe now I'd do it differently, but back then I wanted to make my own choices, control my own decisions. The army was *my* choice. Special Forces was *my* choice. And when the Colonel left the unit…following him into Big Sky was my choice, too."

"I get it," Isabella said around the angry lump in her throat. "It was all about what you wanted. I was collateral damage."

He nodded, and Isabella found herself wishing he would look away. His murky-green eyes were too direct, too honest. "I'm sorry about the way it ended. But I can't say I'm sorry it ended. We were too much, Iz. It wasn't healthy."

Heat washed her cheeks at the reminder, at the truth, and she was the one to look away. She stared out the window, down where the clouds had gone from white to gray. "Lucky for us that was a long time ago. We're not dumb kids anymore. Nothing like that could happen between us now."

She meant it as a statement of fact. But somehow, once the words were out there, they sounded more like a challenge.

"Yeah." He turned back to his flying. "Lucky for us."

ONCE THEY WERE on the ground in D.C., Jacob put in a call to Cameron, as much to remind himself of the job as to catch up with any developments. While he waited for the call to connect, he tried to work through the hot burn in his chest.

Anger. He was used to it. He could handle it. Back when they'd been in the Forces together, right after Jacob had been rung up for yet another bar brawl, Cameron had sat him down and talked about anger management. Self-awareness. Control.

It was an odd lecture coming from their warrior of a

leader, but it had resonated. And Jacob, who prided himself on control, realized he'd lost it somewhere along the line. From then on, he'd tried to master the quick slashes of temper, to redirect those energies into motion and action. Games. Sparring. Whatever it took. And for the most part, he'd succeeded in controlling his temper in the years since.

Until now. Sixty hours in the presence of Isabella Gray and he was ready to bite steel in two and howl at the moon.

If that wasn't rage, what was it?

"Murphy." Cameron answered the phone after what seemed like twenty rings.

"It's Jacob. We've landed fine and we're on our way to Cooper's office. Isabella thinks she can get past security." When his boss didn't reply right away, Jacob asked, "Anything on your front?"

"No, nothing," Cam answered with a hint of frustration in his tone. "We got some prints at the clinic break-in. They're a clean match to a pair of Boone's men— Kane Meyers and Ray Fleming. But that's all we've got. Wait…hold on a second." There was the sound of a low, muffled conversation in the background, then Cameron's voice returned, sharper now. "The blood-hounds hit on something just the other side of the ridge. I'm headed up there now, but I'll get you an update as soon as I'm back in cell range."

"Okay. Good luck," Jacob said, trying not to feel cut off from the central action, the main hunt. He knew they needed to work this thing from both ends toward the middle, because there was no telling whether the bloodhounds' scent would pay off. It usually didn't, though Trevor Blackhaw handled the animals as well as anyone.

"You, too." Cam cut the connection, leaving Jacob standing alone in the airport terminal while Isabella and Joseph held a cab outside.

He hesitated, thinking that stepping onto the curb would be like moving backward into the past. He'd spent a good chunk of his teenhood in D.C., after his father made the move to the national stage, and he'd stayed until two weeks after his graduation from Georgetown. After that, he hadn't looked back, hadn't returned except for the occasional holiday with his parents.

But it wasn't their expectations, or their disapproval, that permeated his thoughts of the capital city now.

It was the woman outside. Isabella.

Jacob didn't know what tricky twist of fate had landed them back in each other's orbits, but he knew one thing for sure. Whether she liked it or not, whether *he* liked it or not, the thing that had once existed between them wasn't dead yet. It was alive and well, as though it had simply been waiting all these years, biding its time, hiding until it could leap back out and take over his every rational thought, as it had once done.

Nothing like that could happen between us now, she'd said, and she was one hundred percent right.

It couldn't, because he wouldn't let it. He couldn't afford to get involved with Isabella Gray again, couldn't afford to lose himself.

"So focus on the job and get on with it," he told himself, shoving his cell into his pocket and hefting his duffel.

Just before he stepped through the doors, his attention was caught by a television monitor set high above the lobby of the small private airfield. One of the twenty-four-hour news channels showed a split screen, with Prince Nikolai of Lunkinburg on one side, King Aleksandr on the other.

He couldn't hear what was being said, but he could make a good guess. Nikolai was calling for freedom, his father for the death of anyone who presumed to interfere in what amounted to a brewing civil war.

Jacob felt a hollow clench in his gut as he pushed through the doors, out into the well-remembered east coast air.

This was getting too damned complicated.

THE CAB RIDE from the airport was silent, but charged with tension and things unsaid. Prickles of failure worked their way through Isabella, needling deeper as each mile brought them closer to her condo, where they planned to pick up her car and arm themselves from her rather skimpy arsenal.

She fought the urge to close her eyes against the passing scenery. The last time she'd been in D.C., things had been normal. She'd been protecting Cooper's family and planning for their vacation security.

Now, she was disgraced.

When the cab pulled up outside her place, she hesitated at the curb and glanced at Jacob. Throughout the journey, she had been too aware of his masculinity, too conscious of his every move or expression. On one level, she craved the connection.

On another, she resented it.

"Joseph and I can wait out here." He gestured toward her home, which was half of a refurbished brownstone with the added bonus of a garage that had been attached with fine architectural disregard sometime in the seventies. "Make it quick."

She would have bristled at his tone, but she was too relieved not to have him in her home. That was her space, and the last thing she needed was a memory of him to add to the emotional clutter.

So she nodded. "Be right back."

In under five minutes she was pulling out of the garage in the sleek, late-model BMW that was one of her few extravagances. Joseph whistled. Jacob merely lifted a brow.

"Nice wheels."

"They get me where I'm going," she answered, trying not to care that he liked her car.

It took them less than a half hour in midday traffic to reach Cooper's private offices, a suite of rooms he kept away from the public theater. If there were backhanded deals—say, his family's safety in exchange for a vote to keep troops out of Lunkinburg—then they'd be made in the private office.

Or so Isabella hoped, because with her security clearances revoked pending the psych eval, there was no way she was getting near his office in the Pentagon.

When they reached Cooper's private office, she was lucky enough to nab a street space nearby. She left the

BMW angled slightly away from the curb, poised for a quick getaway.

Just in case.

The building was intentionally generic, a gray facade with glass doors opening into a bland lobby. A stranger wandering in off the street would never know that it housed the private office of one of the country's most powerful men. A man who could swing international policy with the direction of his vote.

A man who was in deep trouble and didn't want her help.

She took a breath and pushed through the door, aware of the two bounty hunters forming a tough-guy phalanx behind her.

"Hey, Tom." She waved at the single security guard. "Cooper's wife asked me to drop something off. I'll just be a minute." She jerked her head back toward Jacob and Joseph, who looked inescapably rough and ready, even wearing business casual in place of their jeans and pullovers. "These two will wait out here."

"No problem, Agent Gray." The guard waved her through. It seemed too easy, but Isabella knew the security setup was state-of-the-art. Checks were being run on her as well as facial recognition on the men. She had maybe five or six minutes before they realized she had no authorization to be here.

Plenty of time to do what she needed to do.

She glanced back over her shoulder and saw that the bounty hunters had ranged themselves against the front wall, leaning back amid generic art and uninformative signs. Joseph scowled off into the middle distance, which seemed to be his habitual expression. But Jacob stared back at her, unflinching.

Their eyes met and heat arced across the intangible contact. The breath backed up in her lungs and she nearly missed a step before she forced herself to look where she was going and walk away from him.

We were too much, he'd said. *We weren't healthy for each other.* And part of her knew he was right. She'd spent the past decade avoiding that sort of emotional roller coaster, that manic buzz of sex and confusion.

But another part of her craved the high.

That was the part of herself she feared.

No matter. It wasn't important right now, she told herself. Cooper was the focus. The target. They had to figure out what he knew, what he was doing.

And who was calling the shots.

Knowing that the elevator could be frozen from the security kiosk during an incident, she took the stairs up to the third floor and paused outside the Secretary of Defense's unmarked door. The last time she'd been here was to meet Hope and the girls for a prevacation shopping trip. It was amazing how quickly things had changed.

Heart pounding, Isabella swallowed hard, slipped a small disc from her pocket and shouldered through the door without knocking.

She burst in on a seemingly frozen tableau. Secretary Cooper stood behind his desk, palms flat on the polished wood so he could lean forward and make his point to the man standing opposite him.

Prince Nikolai of Lunkinburg.

Isabella's momentum carried her into the room before either man could react. She stumbled and grabbed for the desk to catch herself. "Oh, I'm sorry. I didn't mean to interrupt."

A dull flush climbed Cooper's face and distress flickered in his eyes, though she couldn't tell if it was born of fear for his family, guilt at being manipulated by Nikolai's father, or something more sinister than either of those things. He masked the expression quickly, blanked his face to a politician's earnest neutrality and straightened himself to his full height.

"Of course you meant to interrupt, though I can't fathom why." His eyes flickered to Nikolai, telling her that the prince had no idea of the abduction, that Cooper had stuck to his plan of following the kidnappers's instructions. "As I told your superior, I'm perfectly safe here in D.C., so there's no reason for you to concern yourself further with me or my family."

On the opposite side of the desk, Prince Nikolai smiled. "Perhaps she was not looking for you at all, my friend." He stretched out a hand. "It's a pleasure to see you again, Agent Gray."

She felt Cooper silently urging her to play along with the sham, and felt the prince urging her to…what? What was the fine tension she felt running between the men? What was the urgency she sensed at the back of the prince's eyes, and the slight tightness at the corners of his mouth?

Did he know something about Aleksandr, about a connection to MMFAFA? Did he know Cooper's wife and daughters were missing, that they'd been taken just before the Secretary of Defense had changed his position on sending troops into Lunkinburg?

Then the prince withdrew his hand and gave her a tired but still-handsome smile, and her quick thoughts collapsed in on themselves.

The prince was a good man caught in the unenviable position of fighting against his father for the good of his people. He was as much a victim of King Aleksandr as Cooper and his family were.

Isabella set her jaw and turned her attention to Cooper. "I came to ask you to reconsider your decision. The threats are viable. Your family could still be in danger."

She let Nikolai think she was talking about the threatening letters the Secretary of Defense had received before his vacation, knowing that Cooper would read the subtext. *Let me help you. It doesn't have to be this way.*

Cooper's neutral expression chilled. "I told you before that I don't need your help." He crossed the room and held the door open, shoulders tense with anger, or maybe guilt. "Please leave."

She inclined her head as she stepped across the threshold, but held his eyes, silently urging him to accept her help. "You have my cell number if you change your mind."

"I won't," he said sharply, and shut the door behind her.

But it didn't latch.

Aware of the hallway cameras, of the minutes ticking and the increasing chance that the building security forces were even now realizing that she had no business near Cooper's inner sanctum, Isabella leaned back against the door and strained to hear the men's conversation.

"...can't believe she barged in here like that!" snarled Cooper, tense and anxious.

The prince's lower, soothing accents returned, "She was only doing her duty. You should be grateful for such loyalty." His tone darkened. "I know I would be. But given the number of my friends who have proven bound to the king..." He sighed. "Loyalty is important in this day and age."

The words sliced at Isabella. Duty. Loyalty. Two things she'd always prided herself on, perhaps foolishly so.

"True, but so is following your heart," Cooper answered, leaving Isabella to wonder whether the statement had more than one layer.

"Yes," the prince agreed, "we've made a great deal of progress. But—" now his voice hardened and his accent deepened the words to a growl "—we cannot let anything—or anyone—interfere with the possibility of restoring peace to Lunkinburg."

Silence thundered in the room after that declaration. It took Isabella a moment to realize that the rumble wasn't silence after all, but rather the ring of boot steps on the far staircase.

Her pulse accelerated.

The guards were coming for her.

Time to go!

DOWN IN THE LOBBY, Jacob tensed when the kiosk phone rang. The lone guard answered, listened for a few seconds, then replaced the receiver. He didn't look toward the bounty hunters, but Jacob could tell they were the focus of the guard's peripheral vision.

"Problem?" Joseph murmured out of the side of his mouth.

"Maybe." Jacob glanced around and didn't like what he saw any more than he had the first time he'd scanned the small lobby.

The front door was the only way in or out unless they could get past the security desk. And he was betting two things—one, that the guard had backup, and two, that the guy had a small arsenal within easy reach.

He cursed himself for not having insisted that Isabella prep them on the setup more fully. He'd stupidly assumed it would be an easy in-and-out.

He'd been wrong.

Below audible hearing, he felt the vibration of running feet. Of pursuit. His heart kicked up a notch, his body tensed for action.

Isabella can take care of herself, he told himself, *she's a trained agent.*

But though he'd known for years now that she was in the Secret Service, somehow his brain hadn't equated that with her being in danger. Now that the evidence was at hand, he wanted nothing more than to fight his way past the kiosk and beat the tar out of anyone who dared lay a hand on her.

"We leaving?" Joseph asked quietly when the security phone rang again.

"Quietly," Jacob agreed. Every fiber of his being screeched for him to help Isabella, but that wasn't the backup plan.

Worse, he knew if he busted in there and made a ruckus, Cooper was likely to bolt. It was imperative that the Secretary of Defense stay put.

"Off we go, then." Joseph led the way to the door, pulling a pack of cigarettes from his jacket pocket. Jacob knew the pack was nothing more than a prop, a way of saying, *We're just headed outside for a quick smoke,* though for the life of him he couldn't remember whether D.C. had gone smoke-free yet.

Then the outer door opened and Joseph stopped dead. Jacob nearly rammed into him from behind.

"Mr. Brown? Is that you?" a softly accented, feminine voice inquired. "What are you doing here?"

Joseph's already tense frame froze to granite.

Jacob moved to stand at his friend's side, and paused at the sight of a delicately beautiful blonde in her mid-twenties. More specifically, he paused at the sight of the bodyguards flanking her and the sparkle of state jewels at her throat and wrists.

Princess Veronika Petrov of Lunkinburg. Nikolai's sister.

What the hell was she doing here?

The bubbly blonde smiled up at the scowling bounty hunter. "I'd be suspicious that you'd followed me here from Montana, except that I didn't know we were coming here until the last minute. In fact, we've just arrived!" She smiled wider, encouraging him to respond.

Incredibly, Joseph's habitual frown softened a little

around the edges. "Business, Princess," Joseph said, his voice thicker than usual. "We're here on business."

"And we need to go," Jacob interrupted. "Sorry."

He grabbed Joseph and they hurried out onto the street just as the security phone rang a third time and the guard reached beneath his desk, presumably for a weapon.

"Come on," Jacob said urgently, "we need to get the car and meet Isabella at the pickup spot."

But Joseph glanced over his shoulder, face thoughtful. "Let's split up. I have something I need to do."

He was gone before Jacob could argue. Moments later, the BMW screeched to a halt at the curb. The passenger door banged open and Isabella shouted, "Jacob. Get in!"

He barely paused to feel the wash of relief that she was safe. Then a dark green sedan sped around the corner and accelerated.

Oh, hell. They had company.

"Get in, now!" she nearly screamed.

Jacob leaped into the passenger seat. Even before he'd banged the door shut, Isabella stomped on the gas, cut back into traffic and blatantly ran a red light, weaving in and amongst the beeping, bleating early afternoon traffic.

Jacob strapped on his belt, then risked a look behind them.

The green sedan was right on their tail.

And gaining.

Chapter Seven

Stupid. How could she have been so stupid?

Isabella kept the gas pedal jammed nearly to the floor, gritted her teeth and cranked the steering wheel to the left, aiming them down a two-lane crossroad. The wheels chirped and the passenger side left the ground for a second, then two, then slapped back down onto the pavement and they were through and accelerating.

She let out a sharp hiss of relief and shot a glance at Jacob, who was braced in the passenger's seat, arms and legs splayed against the floor and door frame.

His teeth flashed against his tense face. "Just think of me as ballast."

The words were light, though his tone was anything but. And he had a point—without him in the car, she probably would have flipped over.

But she couldn't think about that now. Not with the speedometer edging toward sixty and a T intersection up ahead.

"Hang on!" She breathed a quick prayer, tapped the

brakes and sent the car into a controlled leftward skid. Her heart jammed her throat when the back bumper clipped a curbside light post. The whole vehicle jolted and shimmied nearly out of control. "Hang on, baby. Hang on!"

She hoped Jacob realized she was talking to the car, not him.

How had she let this happen? How could she have been so arrogant as to think the kidnappers would let her waltz into and out of Cooper's private office? And once they'd discovered her and chased her out of the building's back exit, why hadn't she left Jacob behind and led the pursuers away?

A glance in the rearview mirror showed her that the green sedan was half a block behind. A glance to her right showed Jacob bracing himself backward in the seat with his gun in hand.

That was why, she thought. She'd needed her one-man army.

He met her eyes briefly. "Let them catch up."

"With the way I'm driving, there'll be cops here any minute," she said, zigzagging in and among the traffic and swerving down another cross alley. "And no cowboy stuff. I don't want anyone hurt."

"Me neither." He pressed the button to lower the window. "So get us someplace nobody will get hurt."

They broke out of the alley and she slung the car right, toward a more open road leading out of the city proper. "I know just the place."

"I hope it's close. They're gaining."

She didn't bother looking into the rearview. She

knew the green sedan was getting closer. She could feel it, just as she could feel that the men behind the dark-tinted windows meant to kill them.

They weren't part of the office security detail, she was sure of that much. So who were they? Did they work for the kidnappers? For the despotic king of Lunkinburg? For Boone Fowler?

Or all of the above?

"There." Jacob pointed at a large parking lot adjacent to new construction.

"I know." She sent the car screaming into the lot and swerved around to the back of the half-finished building. The megamart was being built to replace a fire-gutted strip mall, but right then, it was lunchtime quiet.

Or had been.

The green sedan spun in behind them, sliding nearly sideways before its tires bit into the pavement and shot the vehicle in pursuit.

"Now let them catch up," Jacob said calmly.

Isabella eased up on the gas, enough so the green car could close the gap, not enough that it would seem deliberate. She glanced over and saw a glint of approval in Jacob's eyes, quickly masked by determination as he braced his shoulders against the dashboard and leveled his weapon out the window. "Hold her steady for me."

"Leave them alive for questioning," she said quietly, her attention fixed on the tarmac ahead. "And whatever you're going to do, do it fast. You've got about five seconds before I run out of pavement and we make a hard left."

"Gotcha."

"And don't miss."

He snorted. "Babe, I never miss."

Incredibly she felt a little lift beneath her heart at the careless endearment. She squelched the feeling as quickly as it had come, but the fact remained.

She was coming to care what he thought of her again.

Or else she'd never stopped caring. And that was a hell of a thought.

Then she couldn't worry about it, because the sedan's driver, or maybe a passenger—she couldn't tell through the tinted glass—opened fire.

Isabella screamed and jammed her foot on the gas, wanting out of here as fast as possible.

"No!" Jacob shouted. "I can do this!"

Then he had no choice. A line of bullets stitched its way across the trunk of the BMW and spiderwebbed the back window. .

"Right! Turn right!" Jacob braced himself for the swing. "I need a clear shot!"

She yanked the steering wheel hard, cursing when the tires hit a patch of sand and slid. Bullets smacked into the side of her car—the one she'd scrimped and saved to buy—and Isabella set her jaw, waiting for the pain of a hit or for Jacob's cry.

Instead she heard a single gunshot from the passenger side. A low word of triumph.

"Bullseye."

The car lost its grip on the oily patch of sand and spun in a one-eighty that left Jacob and Isabella facing their pursuers.

The green sedan closed on them, racing for a head-on collision.

Then, incredibly, the car swerved sharply to the left and crumpled forward as the front axle snapped. The driver's front wheel jammed, but the vehicle's momentum continued.

Metal screamed and the vehicle exploded off the ground, the back end flipping up and over the front. Only one front wheel was jammed, and the resulting torque spun the sedan in an aerial cartwheel of crashing metal and flinging fragments. The green sedan flipped lengthwise and slammed into a half-wired lamppost, which folded with a snapping groan and landed on the car with a crunch of metal and safety glass, then lay still.

Dead still.

Isabella cut the BMW's engine and winced at the sudden, deafening silence.

"What are you doing?" Jacob demanded. "We need to get out of here while the getting's good!"

"What we need to do," Isabella replied as she unbuckled her seat belt with adrenaline-numbed fingers, "is question whoever is in that car. If we figure out who they're working for…"

She trailed off, but the answer crackled on the still air between them. *If we figure out who they're working for, we'll know who to go after. Maybe even where to look for Hope, Becky and Tiff.*

She swung out of the bullet-riddled car with Jacob's soft curse following her. She hadn't gone more than three steps toward the green sedan before he was at her side. He grabbed her elbow and hurried her along. "Come on, quick in and out. Or do you *want* to hang around and chat with the cops?"

She heard it then, the muffled rise and fall of approaching sirens. She tensed. "I'm not afraid of the police. I'm a Secret Service agent."

Then she gritted her teeth on the slip. She *had* been an agent. Now she was nothing. Cut loose, cast adrift. Alone.

"Hey." Jacob nudged her with his elbow and jerked his chin at the green sedan. It lay on its roof, three wheels still spinning gently, the fourth twisted and hanging from where his single shot had blown out the tire. "You coming?"

She focused on him, on the sweep of his jaw and the wide set of his shoulders, and felt for the first time since she'd knocked on the front door of the bounty hunters' log cabin, that she'd come to the right place.

To the right man.

And that complicated more things than it solved.

Unable to deal with the thought just then, she nodded. "I'm right behind you."

But when they reached the crumpled vehicle, Jacob stopped dead and cursed under his breath.

Isabella crouched, expecting to see that their pursuers were unconscious or worse, dead. But the sight that greeted her eyes was surprising and even more unsettling.

The green sedan was empty.

She stood and scanned the scene. Her stomach knotted at the sight of a blood trail leading to the deserted main road beside the parking lot.

There must have been another chase car. A backup. A getaway.

Which left them with nothing.

"Come on." Jacob tugged at her arm. "Company's coming, and there's nothing more we can do here without getting involved with the officials."

And that would just slow them down when they could least afford to be slowed.

Stunned by the chase, the accident and the fact that their pursuers had escaped, Isabella allowed him to point her toward the passenger's seat. He took the wheel and they sped from the deserted parking lot moments ahead of the lone cop car with its flashing lights.

But though the single car was first on scene, Isabella knew the place would soon be jammed with personnel. Car chases and gunfights weren't unheard of in the nation's capital, but they were taken very, very seriously.

"We need to ditch the car someplace safe," Jacob said, his thoughts clearly paralleling hers. "Between the bullet holes and the shot out back window, there's no mistaking what we've been up to."

"And she's registered in my name," Isabella said sadly, hating the mess the men had made of her pretty BMW.

The mess they'd made of her life.

Unexpectedly, Jacob reached across the space between them, took her hand and squeezed. "Sorry."

"It's not your fault," she said automatically, even as warmth snuck up her arm and wrapped itself around her heart. "Turn here." She indicated a back road that paralleled the main highway. "I know where we can go."

She kept them on the quieter back roads and hoped nobody called 9-1-1 about the obvious bullet marks on

the car. By the time they reached their suburban destination, it was midafternoon, though it felt as though a
week had passed since they'd landed the jet that morning.

"Pull in here." She indicated a generic two-level
town house in the midst of a cookie-cutter development, where each house perched atop a two-bay garage.
"I'll get the door." Without waiting for his answer, she
hopped out—keeping a sharp eye on their surroundings—and punched in the door code.

Once the bullet-riddled BMW was inside, she closed
the door and dropped the blinds on the high windows,
just in case.

When she turned back, Jacob was standing too near,
his eyes hooded. "Whose place is this?"

She fought the insane urge to step back, away from
him and from the intensity that seemed to pour off him
in waves. "It's not connected to me in any way. They'll
never think to look here."

He glanced around at the garage, and she saw his
eyes linger on the sports equipment and the shiny
chrome of a bike with a naked woman's silhouette em-
blazoned on one side. His lips tightened. "Your boyfriend's?"

She nearly snorted at the thought, but held it in,
partly because it was none of his business and partly because it might be safer if he thought she was involved.
Then she thought, *Safer for whom?*

She turned and popped the bullet-dented trunk. "This
is Lance Drummond's place. He's Secret Service, and
out of the country for another week. We're..." *Friends,*

she started to say, then stalled when she realized that wasn't even close to accurate.

"Never mind. I get it." Jacob reached past her to snag the two carry-on suitcases they'd brought with them.

"No," she said quietly, "you don't." When his eyes met hers, she shrugged. "I wouldn't even call Lance and me friends. His girlfriend dumped him just before he left. I was standing there in the hall when it happened, and he...I..." She swallowed a bubble of nervous laughter because truth was so very pitiful, and rushed through it on a single breath. "He asked me to water his plants."

And this had been the best place she could think of to hide. Jeez, she should've just tattooed "pathetic" across her forehead. She jammed her hands into her pockets and told herself to get over it. Since when did she care what anyone else though of her or the way she chose to live her life?

Since she'd gone looking for Jacob Powell, that's when.

Instead of looking relieved, or pitying, he nodded. "Good. Then we should be safe." He turned away. "Come on. We have surveillance to set up." He hefted the silver suitcase that contained Big Sky's bugging equipment. Then he paused and his eyes sharpened on her. "You planted the receiver before they chased you out, right?"

She thought back to those first few tense moments in the Secretary of Defense's private office, when Cooper and Prince Nikolai had watched her so closely—

And she'd pretended to stumble and catch herself on the desk.

She nodded slowly. "The bug's in place."

"Good." He grinned, a surprising flash of white against the dim light of the garage. "Then let's get these bastards."

ONCE THEY WERE INSIDE the six-room town house— *Lance's* town house, Jacob growled internally, not sure that he bought the plant-sitting excuse and trying to tell himself it didn't matter one way or the other—they set up the surveillance equipment they'd brought from Montana.

If they were very, very lucky, the bug in Cooper's office would give them a clue as to where his wife and children were being held, where a ransom drop would happen...or even who was masterminding the plot.

Because the more Jacob thought about it, the less likely it seemed that Boone Fowler was acting on his own. It wasn't just that the scheme had international implications, it was the *feel* of the incidents.

Boone normally worked near his roots in Montana. The danger had followed Jacob and Isabella to D.C.

The MMFAFA focused on domestic terror. Cooper's flip-flop on the Lunkinburg policy suggested pressure was being applied from without.

And wouldn't logic say that Boone and his men would lie low after escaping from The Fortress?

"Hell," Jacob muttered under his breath. "It doesn't add up unless there's someone else involved."

Someone like King Aleksandr.

"What did you say?" Isabella asked, reentering the room with a pair of sodas and an open bag of chips, which she placed on a nearby table.

"Nothing." He deliberately turned his attention to the portable surveillance equipment, but his every sense was attuned to her presence, to her movements, to her small hiss of frustration when he shut her out.

Why didn't she get that it was for both their protection?

He was in a good place now, a calm place both professionally and emotionally, and he'd worked hard to get there. And though he'd glimpsed a spark of loneliness or something darker in her eyes when she'd spoken of her work and her life, he sensed that prior to the incident with Cooper, she'd been content. Settled. Two things they had never been together, when they'd come together in flash and flame and all-consuming, greedy need. He hadn't been able to handle the intensity as an almost college grad and he had no intention of finding out if he could handle it now.

He was pretty sure he already knew the answer to that.

"You all set up?" she asked from way too close behind him.

Jacob stiffened reflexively and stepped away from the bugging equipment, ticked by his body's instantaneous response every time she came near.

"Yeah." He jammed his hands into his pockets. "We're ready to go live."

But *live* was an overstatement once they flipped on the receiver and heard only dead air.

We'd like to send you two free books to introduce you to our brand-new series – Harlequin® NEXT™! These novels by acclaimed award-winning authors are filled with stories about rediscovery and reconnection with what's important in women's lives. These are relationship novels about women redefining their dreams.

THERE'S THE LIFE YOU PLANNED. AND THERE'S WHAT COMES NEXT.

THE EDITOR'S "THANK YOU" FREE GIFTS INCLUDE:

▶ Two BRAND-NEW Harlequin® Next™ Novels

▶ An exciting surprise gift

YES! I have placed my Editor's "thank you" Free Gifts seal in the space provided at right. Please send me 2 FREE books, and my FREE Mystery Gift. I understand that I am under no obligation to purchase anything further, as explained on the back and opposite page.

PLACE
FREE GIFTS
SEAL
HERE

356 HDL D736   156 HDL D72J

FIRST NAME	LAST NAME

ADDRESS

APT.#	CITY

STATE/PROV.	ZIP/POSTAL CODE

Thank You!

The Reader Service — Here's How It Works:

Accepting your 2 free books and gift places you under no obligation to buy anything. You may keep the books and gift and return the shipping statement marked "cancel." If you do not cancel, about a month later we'll send you 3 additional books and bill you just $3.99 each in the U.S., or $4.74 each in Canada, plus 25¢ shipping & handling per book and applicable taxes if any.* That's the complete price and — compared to cover prices of $5.50 each in the U.S. and $6.50 each in Canada — it's quite a bargain! You may cancel at any time, but if you choose to continue, every month we'll send you 3 more books, which you may either purchase at the discount price or return to us and cancel your subscription.

*Terms and prices subject to change without notice. Sales tax applicable in N.Y. Canadian residents will be charged applicable provincial taxes and GST.

If offer card is missing write to: The Reader Service, 3010 Walden Ave., P.O. Box 1867, Buffalo, NY 14240-1867

BUSINESS REPLY MAIL
FIRST-CLASS MAIL   PERMIT NO. 717-003   BUFFALO, NY

POSTAGE WILL BE PAID BY ADDRESSEE

THE READER SERVICE
3010 WALDEN AVE
PO BOX 1867
BUFFALO NY 14240-9952

NO POSTAGE
NECESSARY
IF MAILED
IN THE
UNITED STATES

They listened for a minute before Isabella whispered, "Do you think the bug's malfunctioning?"

"It's not a speaker phone, Iz. You can talk normally," he said a little too loud.

She jumped, then chuckled at herself. "Right," she said, not whispering now. "Sorry. I'm not usually asked into the surveillance jobs." Before he could ask why, or why the fact brought a hint of temper to her expression...and a glimmer of vulnerability, she continued, "Can your equipment tell you if the bug's functioning properly?"

"Yes, it can, and yes, it is," he answered. "But we lost time with those bastards in the green car." His gut clenched at the memory of what had happened. What could have happened if she'd been a less accomplished driver, or if he'd missed shooting out the sedan's front tire.

It didn't bear thinking about, because she was a good driver, and he never missed, and because of it, they'd survived.

This time.

"So Cooper's gone home, or to his other office." Isabella jammed her hands into her pockets, mimicking Jacob's posture.

"Probably," he agreed. "Surveillance can take hours. Days. We should hunker down and get comfortable."

"You might have days to waste on this, but I don't," she snapped, yanking her hands out of her pockets and rounding on him as though looking for a fight. "Hope and the girls don't have the time. We need a break and we need it now!"

His temper surged to match hers, just as it always had. "Then I'll call the local sub shop and order you a break, how's that sound? Maybe a pepperoni pizza with a side of confession?"

Even as he let the words fly, a part of him regretted it, knowing she would respond in kind and the fight would escalate from there. Granted, a good shouting match might clear the immediate tension between them, but it would only emphasize the problem.

They did everything with their emotions turned up too loud.

He braced himself for the explosion, for the fine whip of her temper and the glorious snap of her eyes and voice.

Instead, incredibly, she chuckled.

In her eyes, he saw…not temper, but a reluctant amusement. Something he'd never experienced from her.

Something he'd never expected to.

"Yeah, I guess I deserved that." She picked one of the sodas and tossed it to him. "You're right, it could be a long night. Let's get comfortable."

Jacob caught the can automatically, but his brain was jammed on the look in her eye. Humor, not anger. A hint of accessibility rather than a prickly barrier. Without thinking, he blurted, "Who are you and what have you done with the real Isabella Gray?"

She straightened abruptly and the amusement drained from her face, to be replaced with weary resignation.

"Jacob, it's been, what? Twelve, thirteen years?

Don't think you know me now because we slept together for a few months at the end of college. I'm a different person now." She took a step closer and lifted her chin in challenge. "Aren't you?"

He thought about the work he'd done to control his temper and nodded. "Yeah, I'm different."

"Good." She dropped her chin a notch and linked her hands loosely in front of her, as though she wanted to do something with them but wasn't quite sure what. "Then I think we should try to approach this as though we'd just met."

"That's not a good idea," he said flatly.

"Why not?"

The devil possessed him, or maybe a saint, because when he answered, the words were the honest, unfettered truth. "Because if we'd just met, I'd want to seduce you, and we both know that's a recipe for disaster."

The bald statement hung between them for a long moment. The air seemed to thicken with it, but Jacob didn't wish it back. Better to have things out in the open than festering and causing yet more tension.

Isabella blew out a breath. "Whew. Nothing like going for the jugular, eh, Jacob?" She gripped her hands tighter, her only outward sign of agitation. "And what if I said I'd probably seduce you right back?"

Jacob's gut knotted on a flash of heat and he swallowed. "Then I'd say it's lucky that we haven't just met, because we're here to do a job, not…" He thought to make his point by using a crude word for the act, but couldn't bring himself to do it, so ended with a lame, "Not become involved."

"Lucky," she agreed, but she didn't break eye contact, and he wasn't sure what he read in the depths of her expression. It wasn't vulnerability and it wasn't a barrier of anger.

It was, perhaps, a challenge.

That, more than anything she'd said or done since re-entering his life two days earlier, told him just how much she'd changed over the years. And damn, it confused him.

If she'd changed, maybe he had, too. Maybe he could handle it this time. Handle her.

He took a step toward her and lifted his hand, unsure what he wanted to say, unsure whether she'd want to hear it.

At that moment the bug crackled to life, making them both jump.

In the heavily charged air of a stranger's town house, they heard the sound of a door open and close. The measured tread of footsteps on carpet and the creak of an office chair.

Isabella gestured, and when Jacob glanced at her, she pointed to the equipment and mouthed, *Are we taping?*

He didn't bother to remind her there was no need to whisper, because he felt it, too. The expectant hush of a possible break.

So he nodded. Yes, they were taping.

The minutes ticked by in a frozen tableau. The silence in the town house was broken only by the pop and fizz of Isabella opening her can of soda. The silence in Cooper's office remained unbroken until the phone rang.

Jacob covered a flinch. Isabella started and the air sharpened with intense focus. Jacob imagined she was thinking the same thing he was.

Let this be a break.

The phone rang a second time before they heard the digital beep of it being answered, then a deep, male voice say, "Louis Cooper here."

Jacob stared at the speaker, willing the conversation to be important. Informative. He was conscious of Isabella at his side, barely breathing.

"Damn you," Cooper said, his voice a tortured growl, "where are they? If you've even touched a hair on one of their heads…"

He paused, and in the hissing silence Jacob felt Isabella move to his side. She took his hand and gripped so hard he could feel the imprint of each separate finger on his flesh. He squeezed back, which startled her. She looked down quickly at their joined hands, dropped the contact and stepped back. "Sorry."

The word was no more than a whisper, but Jacob had no time to consider the touch, or its meaning, because Cooper spoke again, clearly responding to the kidnapper's side of the conversation. "No! No, don't do that…I'll cooperate, I swear it." No longer a commanding growl, his voice now edged toward pleading. "Just tell me what to do."

Isabella linked her hands in front of her body and leaned toward the speaker. Jacob jammed his hands into his pockets and forced himself to remain still, though his body thrummed with excitement.

"Wish we'd found a way to bug the phone," he muttered, knowing there had been no way, but jonesing to hear the other side of the conversation just the same.

Isabella nodded quickly, but didn't take her attention off the speaker.

"Okay." And now there was a hint of defeat, of desperation in Cooper's voice. "Okay, I'll be there. The old hangman's cabin in Devil Mountain, California. Monday, noon sharp." He paused and his voice sharpened. "Of course I'll be there. And I get it—no cops. I heard you the first time. Just don't—" his words broke "—don't hurt them. I'll be there. Alone. I swear it."

Bingo! Excitement seared through Jacob at the information, tempered only by frustration that there hadn't been more.

Was this a ransom drop or simply a meeting? Were the hostages being held in the cabin? Damn it, they needed more data.

But they didn't get more. The transmitted silence lasted a long time before they heard the digital beep of a disconnect. Then a thump, as though Cooper had dropped the phone to the desk.

Then broken weeping.

"Aw, heck." Jacob shifted uncomfortably, feeling like an intruder. Cooper's grief tore at him, reminding him that though one of his goals was to retrieve Big Sky's bounty, the more important facet was Hope Cooper and her daughters.

And Louis Cooper, who loved them so much he would—apparently—compromise his principles and change national policy to ensure their safety.

Love could make a man do crazy things, Jacob knew. Like give in to blackmail.

Or join the army.

Annoyed, he shoved away from the dining table that held the surveillance equipment. Away from the sound of a strong man's sobs. "I'm going to scrounge some real food." He glanced back at the speaker. "Can you turn that down or something?"

The words came out harsher than he'd intended, but when Isabella's eyes flashed in irritation, he didn't bother to explain himself. Let her think the worst of him. It was probably safer that way.

She frowned, but her tone was cool when she said, "When do we leave for California?"

For a crazy moment he thought about leaving then and there, flying them as fast as he could away from the men in the green sedan and hiding them until all this was over, someplace he could keep Isabella safe whether she liked it or not.

But that mad impulse passed as quickly as a heartbeat and he said, "We'll leave in the morning."

"Why not now?"

"Because I don't fly tired," he answered. "And because you've had a tough few days. We can both use the rest."

But as he headed for the kitchen, more to escape the tension than out of real hunger, he had a pretty good idea that there would be little sleep for him this night.

Not with Isabella close enough to touch.

Chapter Eight

When Joseph phoned to say he'd find his own way back to headquarters, Isabella and Jacob decided to catch some sleep. She snagged the guest bedroom and Jacob opted to take the couch. Neither of them felt totally comfortable sleeping in Lance's wide lake of a bed, with its satin sheets and questionable reading material on the nightstand.

But once she'd closed the door and lain down with one of Lance's he-man paperback thrillers, Isabella remained wide-awake.

And twitchy.

She didn't need to look far for the cause of her nerves, but she had no desire to analyze her feelings right then. She needed to blow off some steam. So she leaped out of bed, strode out into the hall…and collided with Jacob.

"Whoa there!" He reached out to steady her and his touch burned her from the point of contact to the tips of her toes and back.

Oh, yeah. That was why she was twitchy.

Jacob.

"I'm going for a run," she announced, needing to be away from him, away from the small confines of the town house, which had started to feel like nothing more than a kitchen, a dining room and a pair of beds.

He moved to block her path. "Bad idea. Or have you forgotten about the armed jerks in the green sedan?"

No, she hadn't forgotten. But in an insane way, they'd started to seem safer than the man who faced her little more than a breath away.

"I need to…" She blew out a frustrated breath. "I need to do something. I'm not ready for bed yet."

Her face heated a degree at how the words combined to sound unintentionally sexual, but either he didn't notice or he pretended not to. "Read a book."

She lifted her chin and decided she didn't care how it sounded when she said, "I need to do something *physical.*"

His eyes darkened with irritation and something else. "Fine. Come on."

He turned and led the way downstairs. At first, Isabella thought they were headed for the garage, maybe a nighttime ride on Lance's beloved bike since the car was shot to heck. The idea of riding double on the narrow motorcycle seat held a dangerous thrill—and a chime of warning bells.

But at the end of the downstairs hallway, Jacob didn't reach for the door on the right, the one that led to the garage. He headed to the left.

And Isabella stopped dead. "Oh, no. Bad idea."

Very bad idea.

"You know what's down there?" he asked with a raised brow.

"Of course I do," she snapped, tension forming a tight not in her chest.

She was an agent. Naturally she'd taken a quick look around the town house when she began plant-sitting. It was instinctual for her to note the possible exits, the possible weak spots, just as Jacob had apparently scoped the place out while she'd showered.

Lance's place took up three levels, with the bedrooms on the top floor, the kitchen and living room on the middle floor, and the garage taking up most of the ground level. But not all of it. A small strip of space ran the width of a generous hallway, the length of the entire town house. Most owners in the development probably used it for storage.

Lance had hung a regulation dart board and measured off the lines.

Jacob opened the door. "You said you needed to work off some steam. Come on. What are you afraid of?"

But the look in his eyes said he knew exactly what had her backing off. They'd met over a dart game at Smiley's Pub. She'd hustled Jacob and thrashed him in the first game they'd played, then he'd kicked her butt in the second. By the time they'd played three more, they'd attracted a crowd. Last call came in the middle of their sixth game, leaving them tied at three on the night.

From there, they'd gone back to her place and she hadn't come up for air until three months later, when he'd gone out for a beer and come home with a blonde.

"Are you challenging me," she asked quietly, "or challenging yourself?"

A wry smile tickled the edges of his sensual mouth. "A little bit of both."

She nodded once. "So be it. I think we both have something to prove to ourselves." That as adults, they were stronger than lust, stronger than hormones and flame.

Stronger than need.

But as she followed Jacob down the short flight of carpeted stairs and caught a hint of his male scent in the close air, Isabella wondered whether she was stronger, after all.

He clicked on the overhead lights, revealing what Isabella thought of as "Lance's guy room." The walls were paneled in inexpensive laminate that tried to convey the image of old wood and smoke. A small bar stood at one end of the narrow space. The neon sign above a wide mirror was unlit and Jacob kept it that way.

Isabella was thankful. The place already brought back too many memories.

"Flip for firsties?" he asked, reminding her of that first game they'd played, when they'd shot for who would go first and she'd intentionally flubbed the throw to lull him into a false sense of security.

Eventually they'd moved to flipping a coin for firsties, because it could take twenty or thirty shots for one of them to miss the bullseye.

Now, he held a quarter in front of her.

She nodded. "I'll call it."

She won the toss, and walked to the end of the narrow room to retrieve the darts Lance had left carelessly strewn in the high-quality board. A scattering of plug marks on the wall suggested he missed the board often. As she pulled the darts free, Isabella fought intense self-consciousness. She could feel Jacob watching her, felt a blush climb her body.

How often had they used a game of odds-'n-evens as a prelude to lovemaking?

Sex, she reminded herself. It had been sex. The love had been more on her side than his.

Squaring her shoulders, she walked to her place behind the painted line. "You call the game."

"Have you kept up your throwing?" Jacob's voice sounded thick.

A knot tightened in her shoulders. In her stomach. She flashed a look over her shoulder. "Yeah, I've kept throwing."

Let him think she still went to Smiley's, or that she played in one of the leagues in town. There was no need to tell him that she threw at home, alone, dart after dart until the restless energy was burned off, until the craziness was held at bay.

Some agents went to the shooting range. She stayed home and threw.

"Then you pick the game."

They played for an hour, giving and taking points, winning and losing games until it was clear that they'd both kept their college skills honed, and then some.

The tension between them ebbed and flowed with the games. One moment Isabella could almost believe that she was playing with a co-worker. A friend she traded barbed comments with, someone who hated to lose just as badly as she did. Then they would come too near each other in passing, or brush fingers when they traded darts, and the banked heat would flash into flame, into the greedy sizzle of want.

Each time, one of them would back off. Sometimes, they both stepped away in silent accord.

This wasn't about seduction. It was about killing time. Killing energy.

Too bad the energy between them refused to be killed.

When they were tied at four games a piece, Jacob glanced at her. "New game?"

"Sure." They both knew they could trade games all night long. Easily falling back into a decade-old rhythm, she asked, "Winner takes all?"

He nodded.

"What's the game?"

"Bull."

She tilted her head. "I've never heard of it."

"It's something we invented at Big Sky." He leaned back against the bar. "Five tosses, five bullseyes. You miss the bull, you lose. You miss the board entirely, you owe your opponent a future claim."

She narrowed her eyes. "What sort of future claim?"

"Could be anything." He shrugged. "At the cabin, we've had claims ranging from barn chores to switching bounties. As long as the Colonel okays the trade, anything goes."

"Hmm." Despite a host of misgivings nagging at the back of her skull, Isabella was intrigued. "What are the rules?"

At the question, he straightened away from the bar and crossed to her. Stood too close and looked down at her. Voice low, he said, "There are no rules." The heat climbed suddenly between them, simultaneously binding and separating them. She planted her feet, refusing to fall back though every cell in her body yammered for retreat when he asked, "You game?"

Instead of retreating she nodded. "Yeah. I'm game."

And the battle was on. It wasn't that they forgot about the danger, Isabella knew. The specter of the green sedan haunted them in the tense set of Jacob's shoulders and the quick jolt of attention each time a car's headlights splashed in the window from the road outside. The memory of Cooper's broken weeping settled on Isabella's heart like a limitless weight. They both knew that the hunt would be on again the next morning.

But this moment, this hour in a narrow dart room, was about the two of them.

"You want to go first?" Jacob offered the darts, his attention seeming focused on her, though she knew he must be as scattered as she felt. One part of her yearned for action, while another longed for distance, for a quiet place to hide from temptation. And still another part of her had found the upstairs bedroom too confining, and had brought her down here. To Jacob.

She could handle this. She was a professional, not some green college kid who thought that a split level in the 'burbs and two-point-four kids equaled the stability her traveling salesman father and bipolar mother had never managed to give her.

So she gritted her teeth and nodded. "Sure."

She took the darts from him, steeling herself against the inner buzz when their fingers brushed ever so slightly, a faint rub of fingerprint against fingerprint, identity against identity.

The words *no rules* echoed in her head as she took her position behind the painted line.

His voice spoke behind her. "Do you remember the night we met?"

"Of course. I also remember the night you went home from a graduation party with someone else." She aimed and threw.

Bullseye.

He pulled the dart from the board to free up the tiny target, and continued as though she hadn't spoken. "You were the most beautiful woman I'd ever seen. Not soft-pretty, but fiery and a little bit edgy, a little bit vulnerable." He paused. "Back then, I never would've guessed you'd end up an agent. But it looks good on you. Real good."

Pressure built behind her eyes, a scream, maybe, or tears. But she shook her head. "Don't mess with me, Powell. You're not going to make me miss."

She proved it by burying her next dart in the bullseye, all the way to the shaft. The power of the throw sang up her arm like madness.

"I'm not messing with you," he said quickly, then rolled his shoulders uncomfortably. "Okay, maybe I am. But what if I wasn't? What if I was trying to tell you that I haven't gone a year without thinking of you, haven't met a woman without comparing her to you?

That I'm sorrier than I can say about how I left things, about how I handled things."

"You've already apologized for that. Apology accepted." Isabella steadied her hand when it wanted to tremble in synchrony with the ache in her chest. "As for the other stuff, I don't believe a word of it. You're just playing the game to win. No rules, remember?" She threw with a quick, vicious twist of her wrist.

The dart hit the edge of the bullseye and quivered there as though wanting to leap away, but stayed put.

"Damn it, don't be thickheaded." Jacob shoved his hands into his pockets and pushed away from the bar. "I'm trying to be serious here. This isn't part of the game. No," he corrected himself, "maybe it is part of the game, or maybe I suggested this game so I'd have an excuse to say some of these things. Maybe I was looking for an opportunity to tell you that whatever was between us back then…it was better than I knew." He turned to face the window, so he had his back to her when he said, "And it's not gone yet, at least not for me."

Isabella let her remaining darts fall to her side. "This is a trick, right? Part of your strategy?"

Never in her life would she have expected to hear such things from him. She'd never even considered it. Sure, she'd kept half an eye on his career, she'd known generally where he was, but that was more self-flagellation than anything, a reminder of what happened when she didn't guard herself, didn't keep herself under control.

It wasn't because she'd retained feelings for him. At least, not fresh, living feelings.

Not like the feelings that ricocheted through her chest when he turned back to her, eyes hot and dark. "What if it isn't a strategy? What if seeing you again has brought it all back? What if I'm starting to wonder if I like this feeling? If I need it?"

"And what if you keep asking these questions of me because you're not sure yourself?" she replied, realizing that all his what-if questions were nothing more than defense.

She expected another question in return, or an evasion. So she was unprepared when he dropped all pretenses and looked at her with raw, naked hunger. With all the emotions she remembered from before, magnified tenfold for each year they'd been apart, for each lesson they'd learned separately.

She handed him the darts. "Your turn."

Perhaps a stronger woman would have suggested they go upstairs and face each other across the wide glass coffee table for a discussion. But Isabella wasn't that strong. She wanted the structure of the game, the activity they'd chosen to blow off some steam that had created more instead.

When he took the darts, their fingers brushed in a slow slide, an almost sensual touch of ridge and valley, callus and softness.

The not-quite-caress rocked straight to Isabella's core.

They moved apart in unison and Jacob took his place behind the line. Isabella leaned against the wood-and-chrome bar, her elbows on the polished surface. She imagined she could feel a trace of lingering warmth from Jacob's body.

Headlight beams speared through the single window and they both eased out of the line of sight to watch the car pass without pausing.

Instead of diffusing the tension between them, the reminder of danger heightened the crackle in the air as Jacob aimed and threw.

Bullseye.

He sent her a sideways glance. "You going to talk to me, or are you chicken?"

When he turned his back to her and aimed again, she dug her fingers into her palm. No, she wasn't a coward. But the questions and accusations cramming her brain weren't productive. They were old history, old heartaches. Not relevant to the present.

So she pushed away from the bar and took a step forward. "I'm just trying to lull you into a false sense of security."

He grinned and turned back to the board. Lifted his second dart.

"If you could go back to that night," she said, and saw his shoulders tighten, "would you do it differently?"

A muscle at his jaw bunched and flexed. He threw. Bullseye. He didn't lift the next dart immediately. He stayed facing the board, but answered in a low voice, "I don't know."

Her heart broke a little at that, though she wouldn't have believed him if he'd said yes.

Without waiting for her response, he continued, "You'd said something about a ring earlier that day, like you were expecting one for graduation. I panicked. I got a little drunk and took Brandy Carlisle home with me."

Hearing the name after all these years fisted Isabella's stomach, though she knew it hadn't been about the girl. It had been about them. Specifically, about Jacob finding a way to leave her. But she forced her lips to twist into a half smile. "A *little* drunk?"

"Okay. Real drunk." His third dart buried itself in the bullseye so hard he had to tug twice to pull it free before his next shot. "I needed to be that drunk to invite her back with me." He glanced at her. "I passed out before…you know."

She nodded. "I know. But that doesn't make it any better." He'd intended to cheat on her. After years of overhearing her mother accusing her father of roadside flings and her father saying she'd driven him to it, the intent to cheat was enough for Isabella.

And Jacob had known it, the bastard.

A low fire kindled in her belly, more wrenching than irritation, more all-consuming than anger. "You drove me away because you didn't have the guts to tell me it was over, just like you didn't have the guts to tell me all along that there wasn't a future for us, that you'd planned on leaving just as soon as the ink dried on your degree."

He threw two more darts in quick succession, burying them in the red bullseye. Then he turned to her, eyes dark with anger, and maybe something else. "I didn't plan anything, don't you get it? I never had a chance to plan anything." He advanced on her and gripped her upper arms in his warm, calloused palms. "It was all planned for me. I went to Georgetown because it was expected. I applied to law school because it was expected. I even had a summer internship lined up for me—all part of my parents' plan to make me into my father. The next generation."

"Poor little rich boy." At the flash of temper in his eyes, Isabella fell back a pace until the solidity of the bar pressed against her lower back, stopping her. Propping her up. Another set of headlights passed by, but neither of them watched.

Instead he handed her the darts without touching her. "Your turn."

They traded places and she threw her five bullseyes. Then he threw his. The silence between them grew thick with unspoken accusations, unanswered questions, and over it all roiled the tense electricity that they couldn't deny but chose not to acknowledge.

She wanted him. He wanted her. But they didn't want to want each other. Not again. Not now. Not this way.

She waited until he'd raised his final dart in the set before she asked, "Did you love me back then? Or was that my imagination, too?"

He cursed under his breath, not an angry word, but one filled with desperation. With denial. Without looking at her, he said, "I loved you. But I didn't like who I was when we were together. I felt out of control. Short-tempered. Unbalanced." He glanced over at her. "You made me crazy. I don't want to feel that way again. Not ever."

He threw with an angry flick of the wrist. He missed.

Badly.

They both stared at the dart quivering in the faux wood paneling to the left of the bristle board.

Numbed by the word *crazy,* by the way his comments resonated within her skull, Isabella stepped forward, retrieved the dart and took her place behind the painted line.

The street outside was dark and deserted, the narrow space beside the garage hollow and empty even with Jacob standing no more than three feet away.

Damn him, Isabella thought. Damn his ability to put her right back where she started. She should never have come to Big Sky for help. She would have been better off on her own.

If a small voice at the back of her head said that wasn't so, she ignored it and flung the dart with all her strength.

Bullseye.

"I win." She turned to Jacob and lifted her chin in defiance, refusing to let him see that he'd aroused her, hurt her, stirred her up and made her question herself again, all within the space of a single, stupid dart game.

"And I owe you a future claim." He swallowed and shifted so his weight was balanced evenly on the balls of his feet, as though he expected her to throw a punch. "Do you want something from me?"

Under any other circumstance, with any other man, the possibilities might be endless. But with Jacob?

No. Never.

So Isabella forced her lips into a flat line, not quite a smile, not quite a frown. "Not a damn thing." She turned her back to him and headed for the stairs. "I'm going to bed. Be ready to leave at dawn."

If she spent most of the night reading a paperback until her eyes filmed over and her neck cricked in protest, he didn't need to know. And if once the light was off she lay on her side and cursed him for being right, cursed herself for caring, he didn't need to know that, either.

They weren't looking to rekindle an old, failed love affair; they were trying to rescue Cooper's family and capture Boone Fowler and his associates. Once they managed that, she would be reinstated at the Service and she and Jacob could go their separate ways.

Permanently.

On that thought, she closed her eyes in weary resignation, only opening them once when she heard the hum of a car passing by on the road below.

The morning, and their flight to California, couldn't come soon enough.

THEY WERE IN California. At least Hope thought they were. She'd pretended to be groggy coming off the plane—it hadn't been much of a stretch, because she was certain Boone had dosed her coffee with something—and had pretended to fall asleep the moment they pulled out of the airport in the shiny SUV Kane had driven to pick them up.

At first, she'd slitted her eyes and watched the passing signs of Los Angeles. But then she'd fallen asleep for real, and didn't know how long they'd driven when the vehicle bumped and jolted her back to consciousness.

She groaned. God, her head hurt. Then a second rush of wakefulness crashed through her and moved the pain to her heart.

The girls!

She sat up too quickly and nearly passed out, but clawed through the numbness. "My babies. What have you done with them? Where are they?"

Neither Boone nor Kane answered out loud, but Boone reached forward, popped the glove compartment, and withdrew a sleek silver pistol. He lay it on his lap without looking at her, but she got the message as they passed a row of deserted storefronts and traveled higher into the Sierra Nevada Mountains.

Behave or else.

Chapter Nine

The next morning Jacob and Isabella left the shot-up BMW in Lance's garage and caught a cab to the airport. The air between them remained thick with tension— more emotional than sexual.

Jacob had hoped that reminding themselves why it hadn't worked before might help settle the unspoken push-pull between them. Instead it seemed to have made things worse.

So much so that when he climbed into the cockpit, he didn't feel the usual sweep of joy. Instead he felt jittery.

"You want to ride up front with me?" he asked, expecting her to take the farthest seat away from him, four rows back in the Citation's tail.

"Fine." She brushed past him and took the copilot's seat, leaving him to deal with their bags—little more than a change of clothing and the surveillance equipment they would continue to monitor in the hope of learning more about the meeting.

Was it a ransom drop? A rendezvous of colluders?

An execution?

The image of Derek Horton's bloody face and the single bullet hole between his eyes reached up and caught Jacob by the throat, reminding him that this wasn't about sex, wasn't about him and Isabella.

It was about the job. The bounty. The hostages.

And he'd do well to remember it.

On a growl, he stowed the bags and shut the outer door before he joined her in the small cockpit. They sat mere feet apart, but an icy gulf seemed to stretch between them.

He clenched his jaw, donned his headset and ran through a full preflight check before he asked for ground clearance. They were put through immediately, and he sent the jet down the runway a little faster than necessary, climbed a little sharper than needed, hoping the burst of adrenaline would clear her from his brain.

But it was no good. She was still there. Her scent touched his nostrils and invaded the peace he normally found in the sky.

He held out until they were an hour into the flight, some four hundred miles west of D.C. He turned down the gain on his earphones and looked over to where she had laid her head against the seat back and pretended to doze. "You want to talk about it?"

She stirred, tipped down her reflective sunglasses and looked at him over the tops, her green eyes cool. "There's nothing more to talk about, is there? We had a past. We've dissected it until it's more of a bloody mess than it seemed back then. Do we really need to keep going? You wanted out. I didn't. You got your wish and I learned my lesson." She sat back and pushed her glasses tight to her face, so he couldn't see her eyes anymore. "Let's stop fooling with each other's heads and focus on what we're here for. Finding Hope and the girls. Capturing Boone and his men. Period. End of story."

Unwilling to let it end like that, Jacob reached out and touched her forearm where her turtleneck had pulled up to leave the soft skin exposed. "Is that what you want?"

She angled her head as though looking at him, but the glasses shielded her expression. "I want my job back, and I want my normal, ordered, organized life back. Nothing more."

No chaos, he could almost hear her say, no craziness. Which was ironic, because that was exactly what he wanted, too.

And it was exactly the opposite of what they had together.

He held her gaze—or thought he did—for a moment longer before he nodded. "Okay. Consider the subject closed."

"Good." She tipped her head back and folded her arms across her chest as though settling in for a nap. But her breathing remained wide-awake, as did the fine tension in her arms and legs.

Jacob decided it would be best if they both pretended she was asleep. So he turned up the gain on his earphones and concentrated on flying, the one true love that had never challenged him more than he'd wanted to be challenged, never boxed him into a corner or made him feel out of control.

In the air, he was in control.

Then again, he thought as white puffs of spun cotton clouds reeled beneath the plane, flying didn't send a hum of heat buzzing just beneath the surface of his skin and it didn't make him want to laugh and howl simultaneously.

No, he thought, glancing over and catching a glint of sunlight off her auburn hair, Isabella did that for him. Nobody else. Just Isabella.

And the knowledge both humbled him and scared the hell out of him. He hadn't been strong enough to handle it thirteen years earlier and he didn't think he wasn't strong enough now. They were too volatile together, too passionate. Too everything. He'd be better off without her, as he'd been in the past decade. He'd been stable, sensible, predictable, in control.

But damn, he thought as he turned back to the instruments he knew he could control, he was going to miss the feeling of being around her again, the light touch of her scent and the raging, roaring rush he felt when she crossed him, or worse, when she agreed with him.

Damn, he was going to miss *her.*

ISABELLA WOKE when they landed to refuel, and was surprised to realize she'd actually slept. She felt more settled, more centered.

A week earlier Jacob Powell had been nothing more to her than a memory, one that could be pleasant or unpleasant depending on which part of their time together she chose to remember. There was no reason she couldn't put him back in that role once this was over.

Even better, she'd thought through some of the things they'd discussed, and she'd decided she was the only one holding herself back. Once she was reinstated, she was going to make more of an effort to socialize. She would accept every invitation thrown her way and maybe offer a few of her own.

Heck, Lance was single. Not precisely her type, but maybe worth practicing on.

"You ready?" Jacob's voice broke into her musings. She tried not to focus on the strength of the hand he held out to her, or the rough timbre of his voice when he said, "We've got maybe a half hour to stretch our legs and scrounge some lunch while they refuel the jet."

She gritted her teeth as they stumbled down the short ladder together and separated on the warm, open tarmac of the small middle America airport. When she thought he wasn't looking, she scrubbed her hands against her jeans, trying to wipe away the warmth.

Who was she kidding? She didn't want to be with Lance. She wanted Jacob. But she didn't want the craziness he brought out in her.

Damn it.

"You coming?" He jerked his head toward the main hangar as two uniformed, helmeted members of the ground crew advanced on the Big Sky jet.

"Fine." She followed him into the building and ordered fast food off a hanging menu.

As she did so, she became aware of the near desertion of the airport and a tickle at the back of her neck. She glanced around and saw nothing suspicious. Were they being watched? Or was she looking for a distraction, any distraction that would shift her mind away from her flying partner?

When Jacob rubbed the back of his neck, she wondered whether he felt it, too.

"I'm going to call into headquarters," he announced abruptly. He stalked away, leaving her with a half-eaten sandwich in her hand and the twitch of jumpy nerves in her stomach.

She headed back out to the plane, thinking she should power up the receiver and download anything the sound-activated bug in Cooper's office had picked up since takeoff.

As she walked toward the jet, she saw one of the ground crew members emerge from the cabin. He waved and gave her a thumbs-up. "You're good to go!"

Jacob joined her less than five minutes later, locked the door and quickly ran through the preflight checks.

Once they were airborne, he said, "I talked to the boss. They found a trailer in the woods that yielded some forensic evidence. It looks like several men, one woman and at least one child had been there. There were bloodstains, but they looked old."

Bloodstains. Isabella's heart lunged into her throat and she dug her fingernails into her palm to smother a hiss.

He glanced at her. "God willing, the blood is from a previous resident or an older crime by Fowler's men."

She swallowed and pushed aside the images that threatened to overtake her. Hope bound and gagged. Her daughters lying nearby on a stained and soiled mattress, limp with drugs or worse. Louis Cooper tied to a chair, letters written on his chest in blood.

She sensed Jacob had more that he didn't want to tell her, so she forced the words through a throat that suddenly felt sore and scratchy. "What else?"

"Not much." Frustration laced his tone. "The cabin Cooper mentioned is high in the hills, north of a ghost town called Devil Mountain. Most of the stores have moved out, and the few residents keep to themselves." Jacob shifted in his seat and glanced at her. "Worse, most of Big Sky is hung up in Montana. Murphy says there was another incident at the Fortress—he didn't give me the deets—and they've been called in to give testimony on the governor and the train crash. There's no way he can get to Devil Mountain before Sunday night. He'll do his best to help, but until the end of the weekend…"

"We're on our own," she finished for him, feeling a low churn of nerves build over the hum of the jet engines.

Then she realized it wasn't nerves at all.

It was the engines.

Jacob's low curse confirmed the sudden fear that sent spears of adrenaline through her chest and limbs. She whispered, "What's wrong?" as though keeping her voice low would make the rough, shivering, clanking noise stop.

"We're losing power," he said.

She heard a faint drop in engine pitch, felt a slight loss of gravity that lifted her away from her padded seat and tightened the safety harness against her skin.

They were falling.

Heart thundering, Isabella dug her fingernails into

the padded armrests while Jacob barked their coordinates and condition into his headset. When he fell silent, she asked, "Are we going to crash?"

The fear of it, the final fatality of it, sang through her veins like ice. Like fire. Like disbelief. They were going more than four-hundred miles per hour, thirty-thousand feet above the ground. Now twenty-eight. Twenty-six.

Fear paralyzed her limbs, and she thought, *This can't be how it ends.*

"The plane's going down." A muscle balled in Jacob's jaw and his forearms knotted in sharp relief as the yoke pulled against him, the plane fighting to drop hard and fast. "But we're not going down with it. Get the chutes." He jerked his chin toward the back, where their luggage was strapped.

The floor beneath her feet tilted, then tilted more as she struggled to walk the narrow aisle toward the parachute compartment.

It was empty.

Impossible.

Sick fear washed through her. Her hands shook and her knees wobbled, forcing her to grab an empty passenger chair for support.

"You okay back there?" Jacob called, his voice carefully calm.

"The parachutes are gone!" She fought to keep the tremor from her voice, and mostly succeeded. She could handle this. *They* could handle this.

She hoped.

Jacob didn't bother arguing with her, didn't tell her

to look again. He simply said, "Come forward and strap in. It's going to be a rough landing."

There was no humor in his voice at the understatement. Isabella forced herself to look out a window. Through a break in the too close clouds, she saw a scattering of houses. A gray ribbon of road beside a gleaming snake of water.

But mostly she saw trees and hills. Rocks and canyons and treacherous terrain.

A nearly debilitating wave of terror washed through her, along with the thought that she couldn't do a damn thing to save herself. She was trapped in a chunk of metal thousands of feet above terra firma, and she didn't have the controls.

She wobbled to the cockpit and strapped back in with trembling fingers. "You were a hotshot pilot in the army, right? Tell me we're going to be okay."

Over the rush of wind and the ever dropping howl of the jet engines, she heard a squawk of radio traffic and saw a muscle at the side of Jacob's jaw bunch and flex. He acknowledged the transmission, asked a question in a jargon as unfamiliar to Isabella as the Secret Service codes might seem to an outsider, then signed off.

The altimeter dipped beneath two thousand feet and her ears popped hard. He glanced over at her, a quick slide of dark green eyes shadowed with desperation.

"We're going to be okay," he said. "I promise."

She was pretty sure he was lying.

"Hang on," he said. "We're going in. There's a stretch of desert up ahead that should do for a soft landing."

Isabella thought to herself that sand was hard as stone when you hit it going fast enough, but she didn't bother saying it out loud. Instead she folded her arms across her body and tried to stay limp. Let the harness do its work. The more she braced, the more she'd hurt herself.

At least that was the theory.

The engine whirl dropped to nearly subsonic and she became aware of Jacob muttering beneath his breath. Curses, perhaps, or a prayer.

The ground rose up to meet them gently, slowly, as though the landing would be no problem. But Isabella knew they'd stayed in the air so long because the engines had died gradually, maintaining their speed and keeping them airborne.

But that bonus was also a liability. They were still going fast.

"We're coming in hot," Jacob said, confirming her fear. He fought the yoke one-handed while he flipped switches with the other. "I don't think I'm going to be able to reverse the engines once we're down. It'll all be flaps and sand."

He gripped the yoke two-handed, tense and waiting. As the lowest clouds rushed past them and Isabella's stomach lurched up into her throat, she saw that he was absolutely, preternaturally still. His finger wasn't tapping, his foot wasn't jiggling to an unseen rhythm.

A whimper built in Isabella's throat and lodged there, cutting off her breath. Outside the cockpit—which suddenly seemed far too close to the front of the plane, to the approaching earth—she saw a dry, rock-walled canyon. And sand. Lots of sand.

She locked her fingers together and wished she'd done things differently. Wished she'd tried harder to help her mother, tried harder to reconnect with her father when he'd blown back through her life a few years back, then disappeared again on the wind.

Most of all, she wished she knew she'd be missed.

And feared she wouldn't be.

"Hey."

At Jacob's soft word, she looked over. He touched his fingers to his lips and pressed the secondhand kiss to her cheek. "Trust me."

Then he returned his attention to the rising ground and the falling jet, which was still going—Isabella checked and gulped—nearly two hundred miles an hour.

He needed both hands on the yoke, both feet on the floor, but she felt his touch on her skin. It was more distraction than comfort, but it was something.

Knowing it might be the last thing she ever felt, she was obscurely glad it came from Jacob.

"Going in," he said tersely, and she focused on relaxing. On breathing.

On praying.

At the last moment, when the yellow sand rose up to meet them and a line of scrubby trees blocked their path, Isabella closed her eyes tight. Then, when the darkness seemed too final, she opened them again and stared straight ahead, braced for impact.

The jet plowed through the trees without slackening

speed. An explosion of wood and cactus needles slapped the windows and was gone, then they bellied down once, twice, three times onto the sand, each jolt worse than the one before.

Jacob cursed and prayed and fought the yoke, then gave it up when the engines died and the jet bounced in the air one last time. He shouted, "Hang on!" and the words sounded too loud, too frantic in the sudden quiet of their last airborne hop.

Then the jet slapped the sand once more. Wing first. And cartwheeled.

Isabella screamed. The world exploded into a dizzy whirl, counterpointed by howling metal and a muffled shout from Jacob.

The aircraft slewed viciously and went into a flat spin. A wing came free and ripped a section of fuse-lage with it, opening the cockpit and cabin to the out-side world.

Dust and hot air billowed in, choking them and carrying the noise of shredding metal and chaos.

Fear clutched at Isabella's heart with greedy fingers. She gripped the armrests and braced her legs against the floor as her stomach fought to invert itself. To hell with staying relaxed!

Then there was a horrendous jolt, as if they'd slammed into a cement wall, though she hadn't seen a building for miles. Isabella's body whipped against the harness, which cut into her shoulders and upper thighs.

And then it was over.

The roar of the impact and slide gave way to the sound of shifting sand and clicking metal. Isabella's heart beat loud in her ears but everything else seemed unnaturally still.

Outside the cockpit, the sun glared down on an expanse of reddish-yellow sand and scraggly vegetation. In the aftermath of the crash, it appeared unnaturally quiet.

Then Jacob shifted beside her, breaking the moment of peace, the moment of thanks. He pulled off the headset and tossed it behind him, where it landed on a patch of sand bared by a hole in the fuselage. "You okay?"

"Yeah. I think I am," she said, almost surprised. Incredibly, she seemed to be in one piece. Her upper body burned where the straps had held tight, but she wasn't going to complain about that. Her head and neck hurt from that final whiplash, and puking sounded like a really good idea, but other than that, she was okay. "You?"

"Fine," he said, seeming unaware of a fine trickle of blood running down from his temple.

She swallowed and asked, "Should we get out of here? Is the jet fuel going to blow?"

The very thought sent the nausea into overdrive.

"None left," he answered laconically. "Either we were dumping fuel from a leak or the last full tank wasn't full at all and the gauges lied." Their eyes met, the message passed.

"The mechanic." She winced, remembering. "I saw him come out of the cabin, but I didn't think anything of it. The bastard sabotaged the plane."

"We'll talk about it later." Eyes hard with fury, he unstrapped his harness and struggled to his feet. "Come on. I'll grab the emergency kit, you get the portable radio under your seat and let's regroup. Outside."

He took one step toward the back of the plane and the floor tilted down. The cockpit lifted up.

The plane teetered.

He froze.

"Jacob?" She didn't bother trying to keep the quiver out of her voice this time. "What was that?"

"Probably nothing," he said, but didn't move a muscle. Instead he nodded very slightly toward her seat. "I want you to get the radio. Slowly."

She eased forward and grabbed the red plastic box. When she sat back up, the plane shifted again. The tail tilted down another degree and the whole jet slid back a few inches.

Isabella's heart lodged in her throat. She swallowed hard. "As we went in, I saw a canyon."

"Yeah." Jacob's throat worked. "Me, too." He took a breath and leaned toward the front of the plane. "Okay, I'm going to step back into the cockpit. When I do, I want you to go out the hole in the side."

She got it in a millisecond. He was going to counterbalance the plane, keep it from falling while she escaped.

"No way. We go together or we don't go." She dug her trembling fingers into the red plastic case of the portable radio. "I want you to grab the emergency pack right now and we'll get out together. You go, then I go. No heroics."

"Isabella, don't be a—"

Then there was no time for argument. With a shriek of metal and a hiss of sand, the jet broke free and slid backward, gathering momentum as it tilted more steeply by the moment.

"Go!" Jacob grabbed her and flung her through the torn hole in the side of the plane. A jagged shard of metal caught her shirt, her arm. Pain sizzled through her, followed by panic when the fabric caught and held.

The plane dragged her through the sand toward an abrupt drop-off. A cliff. A canyon.

The moment the jet's tail cleared the edge and tipped down into the crevasse, it would all be over.

"Jacob! Help!"

A blur of motion skimmed over her, followed by a spray of sand as he leaped from the plane. "Isabella!"

He flung the emergency pack away and lunged toward her. He grabbed her outstretched hand just as the jet went over.

Pain sliced through her arm and her shoulder nearly tore from its socket. Then cloth ripped and she was free.

The battered jet slid away, tipped up and over.

And disappeared.

Moments later there was a horrendous crash and a puff of dust washed up and over the lip of the canyon.

Isabella lay still, belly down in the sand, and breathed.

Tears leaked from the corners of her eyes. The nausea was gone. The fear was gone. Even the pain seemed far away. The only emotion resonating in her brain was dim surprise.

They'd survived.

She turned her head away from the canyon, toward the man who had saved her.

He was staring at her, his expression one of horror battling with fierce relief, twin to the emotions that burst through her the moment their eyes met.

Maybe she moved first. Maybe he did. Or maybe they moved in synchrony, scrambling to their knees and lunging together to press chest to chest, thigh to thigh.

She wrapped her arms around his waist and clung. He gathered her close, crushing her against the hard planes of his torso. Their bodies aligned perfectly, and she saw the intent in his eyes, perhaps even before he was aware of making the decision.

To hell with history, his expression seemed to say. *This is now! We're alive!*

Her body wept with joy, with the feeling of his arms around her and the warmth of his body filling the empty places. His eyes darkened to a deeper shade of green and he leaned down, giving her time to back off.

She didn't. She leaned in, making it as much her idea as his.

Their lips touched. Clung. Held. Heat rose to join the relief and color her survivor's joy with something more physical. More elemental.

Jacob.

His taste exploded on her tongue, battered her senses and swept away the carefully constructed barriers in her soul with an overwhelming sense of *finally!*

Their tongues touched, met and melded. Jacob groaned, a harsh, needy sound that called to Isabella, to the things she'd told herself didn't matter, like passion.

The sun beat down on them, filtering through the yellow dust cloud lifted by their landing, giving the scene a golden, glorious hue. She let her eyelids ease shut, closing out the yellow light that seemed to hum just beneath her skin, collecting at the points where she and Jacob touched.

This was the thousandth time they'd kissed in their lifetimes, and the first time they'd kissed in this lifetime. In a moment the exquisite sensations had washed away the old, desperate memories and paved new paths of want. She crowded closer and slid her hands up his chest, until she could feel his heartbeat through the fabric of his shirt.

His pulse was quick and excited, like hers.

She let her head fall back in the glory of the warmth they created between them. He murmured his approval and kissed his way down her throat, to the hollow place between her collarbones that had always been her secret erogenous zone.

Nobody else knew about it. Nobody but Jacob.

He dipped his head, cupped his hands around her lower back and placed a single chaste kiss just below the spot.

Isabella's nipples crinkled to hard, wanting buds and she nearly screamed with frustration as the need coiled within her, eager and greedy and mad. She pulled his shirt free from his pants and slid her hands along the strip of bare skin, then grabbed his belt and hung on for the ride.

The slight chafe of sand reminded her of something, something important, but that brief wisp of thought was quickly gone when he flicked his tongue out to lave the skin around her sensitive spot. She clutched his belt, aligning their hips and pressing close, and he murmured encouragement, or maybe a plea.

But pleas were beyond her. Speech was beyond her as her muscles locked tight and the deep pulsing began.

Then he dipped his tongue into the hollow between her collarbones, and all rational thought fled from her mind. The pulses took over her body and soul, and exploded from within, radiating outward in an instant that seemed to last forever.

Isabella bowed her body in his arms and pulled their hips hard together, grinding against him without conscious thought, driven wholly by the sensations cursing through her. She screamed, maybe his name, maybe no words at all, and left herself, anchored only by his strong arms around her waist and the rigor-locked grip she kept on his belt.

It was an incredible physical ride up and over the cliff of pleasure and down into a morass of passion.

Of insanity.

Then the whirling chaos drained, leaving her hollow and shaken. She became aware of the world around her, of the hot sun beating down on her face and on her chest where Jacob had pulled her shirt low.

Oh, God.

Disbelief crashed through her. She was fully clothed. *He* was fully clothed. What had they just done?

No, she corrected herself, jamming her eyelids tightly shut in an effort to shut out the world for a moment longer. What had *she* done?

A hot flush climbed her body and closed in on her soul when the answer emerged, clear and unavoidable.

She had gotten off on nothing more than a kiss. How desperate could she be? She shivered with reaction, with embarrassment, and shivered again when the motion brought intimate awareness of their positions, of his straining erection pressed between them by her hands at his belt, his hands around her waist, as though they had been frozen together, locked center to center.

Horrified, yet acutely aware of his desire and the heat that rocketed between them, she compelled herself to brazen through the awful awkwardness of what had just happened.

She'd gone over the edge, that was what had happened. She'd let the need take control, let the madness rule her.

God.

She forced her eyes open, forced herself to look at him, where he still bent over her, lips near her throat, as though he'd been paralyzed with shock.

His eyes were the deepest green she'd ever seen them, his lips moist and full from their kisses. His lungs labored to fill and clear, each breath shifting them slightly together and then apart in a shallow parody of love.

No, she told herself. Not love. Sex. It was bad enough she'd rubbed on him as though she was in heat. She wouldn't make it worse by confusing chemistry with emotion, sex with love.

She cleared her throat, then fell silent, not sure what she could possibly say to ease the transition back to reality.

The noise seemed to snap Jacob from his daze. He blinked and swallowed. His hands relaxed at her waist, creating precious distance between their bodies.

He swallowed again and said, "Isabella."

That was all, just her name, with his voice caressing each of the syllables as a lover's hands might touch her naked body.

Only this was no lover. This was Jacob.

She pushed away and rocked back on her heels as he did the same. Suddenly self-conscious, she tugged her shirt back into place, trying not to shiver as her fingers brushed across the sensitized skin at the base of her throat. Trying not to remember the feel of his lips there, the feel of the spiraling madness.

"Jacob, I don't know what to say," she began, feeling the hot blush compete with the heat of the baking sun. "I've never—"

"Shh!" he interrupted her sharply, eyes intent on the horizon. "Listen!"

No! she wanted to shout through the tangle of nerves and lingering sexuality, *You listen!* But then she saw a dot on the horizon. Moments later, she heard the low thump of rotors. Relief slapped at her, both that they were saved and that she could duck the awkward moment after. She pushed away from him, scrambled to her feet and locked her knees to keep from swaying on her numb, boneless legs. "That was fast. They must've had a Search and Rescue bird in the area if they followed your mayday that quickly."

Jacob rose and stood beside her as the dot swelled to the outline of a dark helicopter, coming straight for them.

He saw it the moment she did. Without thinking, she reached out and grabbed his arm. "Jacob! It's not wearing Search and Rescue markings!"

In fact, the black helicopter wore no markings at all. And as it swung around to come directly at them, the side door rolled open and a black-clad man stepped out onto the skid.

Holding an automatic weapon.

Chapter Ten

Fear slashed through Jacob. Hell. It wasn't Search and Rescue. It was the bastards who'd sabotaged the plane, come to check on the survivors.

Or to make sure there weren't any.

He grabbed Isabella with one hand and the emergency pack in the other. "Run!"

"The radio!" She reached back, but he pulled her away.

"Leave it. We don't have time!"

They bolted toward a ridge of stony outcroppings, where the desert gave way to the low scrub of vegetation.

They were no more than halfway to the dubious safety of the rocks and brush when the helicopter crested on the far side of the canyon and dropped down, toward the wrecked plane.

"Hurry!" Isabella sped up. "I don't think they've seen us yet!"

Sure enough, the bird dropped down into the canyon, aiming for the shattered jet.

Staggering through sand that went from hardpan to soft mush and back again, Jacob and Isabella dragged each other to the rocks. Once there, he realized the red boulder formation was larger than it had seemed. He spotted a dark crevice and pointed. "Get in the cave!"

Heart thundering, he grabbed her by the waist and flung her up to the nearest ledge. He boosted himself up behind her as she scrambled toward the dark opening. It wasn't quite deep enough to be a cave, but the back of the shallow cavern widened just enough that they could hide from a frontal attack.

Even better, there was a shaft of sunlight at the rear, coming through a body-size crack in the back wall.

That was something, Jacob thought. At least they had an escape route.

Tension laced through his body, the overwhelming need to protect Isabella tangling with the urge to sneak back toward the crash site and identify their pursuers.

Had the jet been brought down by the MMFAFA or another group? Was King Aleksandr involved or was someone else masterminding the attempts on his and Isabella's lives? And how the hell had their pursuers managed to not only identify the jet and their flight plans, but also to sabotage the plane while it was on the ground refueling?

The questions battered at him, wrangling alongside another confusion.

Isabella. Sex. What had just happened between them.

She pressed close to him to peer through the cavern opening toward the crash site, where the helicopter remained out of view within the canyon. "Maybe they'll believe we died in the plane crash."

"Don't get your hopes up." He shifted away from her, all too aware of the pounding arousal from their sandy encounter, all too conscious of the taste of her on his lips, the feel of her on his skin.

The scent of her steeped all around him.

Then the rotor sound deepened and the bird appeared from the canyon. Dark and anonymous and menacing, it hung just above the sand, facing the bright red plastic of the emergency radio and the line of footprints they had gouged in the sand.

Jacob cursed, expecting a strafing run at any moment, half braced for bullets to spew down from the sky.

But instead the dark helicopter landed near the radio. A black-clad figure emerged, silhouetted against the sand and backlit by the sinking sun. Weapon held casually at his side, the man grabbed the emergency radio, tossed it into the chopper and climbed aboard the skid.

The bird lifted off the sand and paused, as though the pilot was waiting for something. Then it spun in a slow arc and headed toward the jumbled rocks.

Isabella reached out and gripped Jacob's hand. "Here they come. But why so slowly?"

Jacob muffled a bleak curse. "They're using the rotor wash to smooth out our footprints. By the time the real Search and Rescue folk get here, it'll look like we never left the jet." The bird neared the lowest rock outcropping and hovered. The dark-suited figure dropped down, then reached up to accept a small pack with the grace of a trained killer.

A trained hunter.

Then the helicopter turned and powered away, leaving the man behind.

"Where are they going?" Isabella whispered. Tension thrummed through her body and into his.

"They don't want to be here when the rescue folk follow my mayday. Hell, they're cutting it close now." He wished he could touch her, comfort her, but now was not the time. He needed to focus on escape. On survival.

On protecting Isabella from the hunter, who held his weapon at the ready as he sprang up to the first rock ledge and disappeared behind an outcropping.

Tension hummed through Jacob. Knowing they only had a few minutes before the man worked his way up to their hiding spot, he reached for the emergency kit. Isabella watched him, eyes dark with questions and stress, and probably pain from the wound in her arm and a dose of fear, as well.

She hid everything except the question. "What's the plan?"

He pulled a flat case out of the bag. "Take this and load her up."

She quickly flipped the lid, then raised an eyebrow at the sight of the sleek 9 mm. "What else do you have in there?"

"Enough." He pulled out a packet of flares and a pressure trigger. "We brainstormed these emergency kits when Cameron first expanded Big Sky, and we've added to them over the years. Most everything in the bag can be used for five or six purposes."

She slapped a clip into the 9 mm and pocketed three

others before closing the case and setting it aside. "And what's our current purpose?"

"We're setting up an ambush," he said, and hoped he didn't sound as desperate as he felt.

He glanced over at her, took in the shadows beneath her eyes and the firm set of her chin, and wished there was another, safer way. But there wasn't. This was the best shot they had at staying alive. Their assailant was keeping below the rock line, offering them no target for a turkey shoot.

He was going to come at them at the last moment. It was what any trained killer would do.

Hell, it was what Jacob would do.

"You want us?" he muttered, gesturing Isabella to stand back. "You're going to have to come and get us."

He set the flares on one side of the crevice opening and the pressure pad on the other, stretched a thin wire between them and gently brushed a handful of sand atop the mess.

It was crude, but it would have to do as a distraction.

"Come on." He mouthed the words, figuring the hunter might be within hearing distance. "Out the back."

A true professional, Isabella didn't hesitate, didn't argue. She shouldered the emergency pack and handed him the 9 mm. Then she stood on her tiptoes and pressed her lips to his in a fleeting kiss that added a hotter note to the energy thrumming through him. "Kneecap him if you can. I want answers."

Jacob nodded. "You got it."

They eased out the back entrance, backing step by step and scanning their surroundings lest the black-clad man sneak up and around them. But Jacob was betting he'd head for the cavern opening. It was the obvious choice for a hiding spot.

The air outside the cavern was hot and dry, though maybe a few degrees cooler than before. The shadows were longer, the sun nearly lost in the sky. *Hurry,* Jacob's internal clock told him. *Don't let this go past dark. There's only one pair of night-vision goggles in the pack.*

Some twenty feet from the cavern exit, he stopped and ducked behind a cluster of rocks. He waved for Isabella to take cover farther away.

If anything happened to him, she would need to run.

Shoving aside that thought, and the rush of emotions it brought, Jacob aimed the 9 mm toward the opening and waited for the flares.

Any. Moment. Now.

Flash! Bang! Orange-yellow light burst from the cavern along with smoke and fumes. The hunter's dark figure emerged, but he wasn't reeling from the fumes as Jacob had expected.

The bastard had a mask on and his weapon at the ready. He aimed and fired. The bullet slammed into the rock wall, sending stinging shrapnel into Jacob's skin.

He snapped off two quick shots and the dark figure dove back into the cavern, which oozed orange flames and smoke.

With a curse and a prayer, Jacob followed. He stayed low and moved fast, pumping two shots toward a hint of motion as he dove into the cavern.

The bullets plunged through a waving curl of flare smoke and shattered on rock.

The smoke was the only motion in the tiny space. Otherwise, it was deserted, save for a broken faceplate that included both night vision and a breathing filter.

Jacob plunged through the smoke and out the far side. He tensed for a shot, for the pain of bullet piercing flesh, for an attack, any attack.

He got nothing. The rocky scree outside the cavern was deserted.

Its very emptiness chased a chill along Jacob's spine.

The hunter had escaped. Worse, he could be anywhere, including sneaking down on them from above.

"You nicked him," Isabella said. She crouched and touched a small, dark smear.

"Probably when I broke his faceplate." Jacob cast around for another spot of blood. He pointed. "There."

They found three more smears before the trail ended at the sand. But there were no footprints.

The hunter had vanished.

Jacob cursed. "We should get moving." He kept his voice low. Though the lack of gunfire suggested the bastard wasn't in the immediate vicinity, they would need to be careful until they pinpointed his location.

Very careful.

"It'll be dark soon." Isabella cast her eyes upward, where the first hints of fiery gold touched the horizon and set flame to her auburn hair.

"All the more reason to put some miles between us and our new friend."

She glanced back the way they had come, toward the canyon and the swept-bare sand between. "We could fortify the cavern and wait for Search and Rescue."

Then she shook her head, blew out a breath and argued against herself. "Bad idea. What if this guy calls the black chopper back?" She turned toward him, eyes dark with tension. "We've got to find someplace safer, more defensible, where we won't be pinned down."

Jacob nodded. "Exactly. And if I took out his night vision, we might be able to get a head start."

It seemed the best course of action. While the phrase "stay by your plane" had been drummed into his skull, his instructors had also allowed that there were times— such as in combat—when staying near a downed plane was the worst thing to do.

This was one of those times.

The black helicopter could return at any moment, with night vision, or worse, infrared scanners that would show their positions once the sun went down and the desert cooled below body temperature.

Staying with the plane was suicide. But was leaving it any better? The hit man was a professional. He would follow them as soon as he was able.

Jacob glanced out the back exit of the cavern, toward the low, rocky escarpment. He tried to picture the land as he'd seen it in those last few minutes before the crash. To the east, the desert had stretched for miles. To the west, sand bordered on rock, which gave way to forest at a higher elevation.

His mental map, along with what he remembered from the flight charts, said that if they headed west and slightly north, a stiff three-day hike would bring them to the highway, and from there to civilization.

And between the crash site and civilization?

He would deal with the hunter as best he could. Capture him if lucky. Kill him if necessary.

Whatever it took to keep Isabella safe.

Convinced it was the right decision, the only logical one, Jacob jerked his head toward the opening. "Let's go."

They didn't discuss their destination as they worked their way across, leaving no footprints on the baked red rocks. The hunter's watching presence sang along Jacob's nerve endings like an itch. Like a promise of violence.

Or maybe it was the sight of Isabella marching westward, trusting him to guard her back. The tense set of her shoulders made him want to comfort her, to pull her into his arms and promise that everything was going to be okay. But the long, lean curves of her legs and hips sparked an entirely different set of urges and images.

She had screamed his name as she had climaxed from little more than his hands and lips. The memory humbled him.

It inflamed him.

And he couldn't do a damn thing about it.

Within a half hour of steady marching, as the landscape darkened from orange to the dark purple of dusk, they reached a sparse forest.

And a river.

Isabella stumbled to a halt and stood, quietly staring down into the sluggish flow.

Shame slashed through Jacob. She was exhausted and injured with the bumps and bruises of the past few days. He should have called a halt sooner, whether or not they still had light to travel by. Yes, they needed to outdistance their pursuer. But it would do them no good if they were too tired to fight.

He moved up beside her and touched her arm. "Let's fill the canteens and push on. We'll camp farther in, away from the water."

A good hunter always checked near water first. And though they hadn't seen or heard their assailant since leaving the crash site, Jacob's instincts told him the bastard was out there.

Somewhere.

So he hurried Isabella away from the river, pausing only long enough to clean the gash on her arm, which was a nasty mess of torn flesh and clear, oozing fluid.

She stood unmoving as he wiped away the scabby sand and splashed cool water on her arm. The surrounding flesh was hot to the touch. Inflammation or a fast-moving infection? He couldn't be sure, but they were in real trouble if it was the latter.

"I'm fine." As though sensing his thoughts, she moved away and tugged her torn shirt over the wound. "Let's go."

They worked their way deeper into the forest. He kept a close eye on her, but her step didn't falter, though her fists were clenched and her jaw set.

The light failed around them, bringing darkness. Not wanting to risk one of the two flashlights in the emergency kit, Jacob took her hand and guided her through the undergrowth, over a landscape made eerie and green by his night-vision goggles. When he saw the thick stand of brush and the shallow place beneath, he nudged her toward it. "We'll stop here."

He guided her into the hollow and followed right behind. The branches closed in around them, forming both a shield and a barrier. He would have preferred to get higher up, maybe atop a rock formation, but Isabella was dragging, whether she'd admit it or not. This would have to do.

Using the night-vision goggles rather than the light, he doctored her arm with antiseptic and a gauze bandage. The tear was jagged enough not to be easily stitchable, but the bandage, coupled with a jab of penicillin, would have to be enough.

She stayed silent while he tended her, while their combined body heat warmed the hollow. Exhausted, she ate the food bar he offered and washed it down with river water from the canteens. But when he spread the lightweight space blanket over her and offered his thigh for a pillow, she touched his wrist.

"Wake me for the second watch."

"Will do," he answered, lying through his teeth. She was ready to drop, whereas he had another day or two worth of energy to call on.

Feeling that energy lag, he pulled off the night-vision goggles and scrubbed a hand across his face, trying to rub some wakefulness into his skin.

"And, Jacob?" Her voice turned serious. "About what happened earlier…"

"Hush," he cautioned. "We shouldn't talk more than absolutely necessary."

It was a convenient excuse. The reality was that he didn't want to talk about the kiss and what had come after. He didn't want her to explain it away as survivor's relief or adrenaline. He wanted to believe that it had been all about him. About them, though he didn't know what to do about the need.

"I know. I just wanted to say…" She trailed off.

"Shh." He touched a finger to her lips. "We'll talk about it when we get out of here. I promise."

Then, unable to help himself, he leaned down and kissed her on the lips. It was a brief kiss, as fleeting as the desert dusk, and equally as powerful.

The sensations rocketed through him. His body howled with the urge to hold her tight and dive in deep. Hot, fiery want reared up and nearly claimed him. But instead of rolling her beneath him and pressing their bodies together with every breath of his being, he guided her head to his thigh and forced himself not to run his fingers through her short, sassy hair.

Now was not the time.

Worse, he was pretty sure there never would *be* a time for them. They were too different, too driven in opposite directions. She was east coast and he was northwest. She was organized government and he was freelance.

And whether she admitted it or not, she was family and he was solitary. That had been true when they had known each other before, and it was still true. People didn't change that much in thirteen years.

So instead of sliding into another kiss, he set the goggles back on and waited for his eyes to adjust to the green-tinted darkness.

Then, he waited for morning.

"WHAT DO YOU MEAN, you're not sure if they're dead or not?" Boone's shout filtered through the locked door and Tiff whimpered in reaction. Hope shushed her.

She and the girls had been imprisoned on the second floor of what looked like a once-nice cabin set deep in the woods. The land rose up behind the house, so the small bedroom actually looked out on turf and forest not six feet below the single locked window.

"It's okay, sweetie. He's not yelling at you," Hope whispered, keeping her voice low. She cuddled her daughters on the narrow bed and strained to hear Boone's side of the conversation. He and the others had congregated in the sunken great room on the ground floor.

"I don't mean to be disrespectful," Boone said in more moderate tones. "But you promised this would be taken care of." There was a pause, then a series of lower comments that Hope couldn't make out.

She ground her teeth in frustration, knowing she needed all the information she could collect.

"What happened? They lose the bounty hunter?" Lyle asked.

"Yes, damn it," Boone's voice replied. "The Secret Service bitch and the bounty hunter went down a few days east of here. It seems they survived the crash."

Isabella was coming! Excitement jolted through Hope and she gripped her daughters tighter until Becky squirmed.

Boone continued, "But don't worry. Our employers are taking care of it. We won't have to deal with anyone except Cooper. He's due here Monday." He chuckled menacingly. "And we all know what to do with him, don't we?"

When the others laughed agreement, fear lanced through Hope. What were they planning for her husband?

Oh, God. She had to escape, had to get away and intercept Louis before he played into Boone's hands.

Hope turned her attention to the screws holding the single window shut.

If there was a way out, she was going to find it and use it to save her husband.

To save her family.

Chapter Eleven

Isabella woke with a jolt, startled by the quick pain in her arm, the solid warmth beneath her cheek and the gentle tangle of fingers in her hair. She sat up too fast and bashed into a low thatch of branches.

The hand that had been stroking her moments earlier—or had that been a dream?—grabbed her and yanked her back down.

"Quiet!" Jacob warned. "And lie still."

She froze, the situation coming back to her in a blink as she remembered the plane crash and the dark hunter. The explosive kiss she and Jacob had shared near the crash site and the way he had refused to talk about it, as though the encounter had meant nothing to him.

Then she realized something else. He had let her sleep through the night. She tilted her head and glared toward his silhouette, which was outlined by the strange purple of predawn. "You were supposed to wake me for a watch."

"I wasn't tired," he said, stifling a yawn.

She should have been annoyed that he'd made the decision for her, but damn it, he was right. She'd been exhausted and needed the down time for some healing. So she nodded, figuring he'd catch the motion, or at least the intent. "Thanks."

He touched her cheek. "You're welcome."

The fleeting brush reminded her that she'd slept on his thigh, curled up near his side, with his arm draped across her, his hand in her hair. Reminded her that she'd slept well, when on any normal night she might have been up pacing.

Reminded her that Jacob Powell was a potent temptation.

She pulled away from him and scooted to the far side of the little hollow, which wasn't nearly far enough. "Have you seen anything out there?"

"Not yet. Now that you're awake, I'm going to go have a look-see." Jacob uncoiled his big body and wormed his way to freedom. Once his feet disappeared from their hiding space, he ducked his head back in, eyes deadly serious. "Stay put, okay? I left you the gun, and there's water in the canteen and food bars in the bag. Go easy, though. We're a few days from the road by my calculations."

Then he was gone with only the faint crunch of footsteps to mark his passing.

Leaving her in the hollow.

Alone.

Without warning, a memory slammed into Isabella. She'd been eight years old, maybe nine, and her father had been home on a brief break between sales trips. She'd been playing outside by herself when he'd appeared, carrying his all-too-familiar suitcase.

He'd leaned down, kissed the top of her head and walked to his car without a backward glance.

He hadn't come back.

Fear ripped through Isabella without warning. Icy panic drenched her arms and legs, leaving her heart to beat crazily inside her suddenly hollow chest. She clenched her teeth around a scream, or maybe a whimper, and willed the emotions away. She clenched her fists and dug her fingernails into her palms as the madness howled through her.

This. It was this she feared more than anything. The mood swings. The near-paralyzing emotion that overtook rational thought, rational response. The doctor said it wasn't clinical, that she had normal responses, normal emotions.

But sometimes she didn't believe it.

Mortified but unable to stop herself, she curled her knees into her chest and wrapped her arms around her shins, as she'd seen her mother do so often. Shutting the world out. Shutting her only child out.

Except that there was no child here, no husband gone on yet another "sales" trip, no suburban house that looked picture perfect on the outside but wasn't.

Here, there was only a carpeting of cold dead leaves.

Here, there was only Isabella.

She sank her teeth into her lower lip and cursed Jacob in her head. Before he'd come back into her life, she'd kept herself level, in control. Her life had been ordered, organized. Effective.

Then she'd gone to him for help and sent herself spinning right back into that crazy place, where she wanted to laugh out loud one moment and scream with frustration the next.

Madness.

Brush crashed overhead. Isabella jerked back and muffled a cry, but it was Jacob's feet that pushed into the shelter, Jacob's body that followed.

And Jacob's eyes that lit on her face and immediately darkened with concern. "What's wrong?"

She dug her fingernails into her palms. "Nothing. What did you see outside?"

"Nothing," he parroted, then opened his arms. "Come here."

She wanted to deny herself the comfort, wanted to deny him the opportunity to give it. Wanted to prove once and for all that she didn't need him, never had. Instead she launched herself at him. Tears burned against her lids, in her heart, and she felt the first of them leak free when his arms came up to close around her solidly, comfortingly, as though he would protect her from everything.

As though he knew exactly what she needed at that moment and would do anything in his power to give it to her.

Isabella knew it was an illusion, that he was no doubt irritated that she'd broken when she so needed to be strong, when they needed to get the hell out of here, stay ahead of their pursuer and get to hangman's cabin before the Monday morning rendezvous. But she let herself cling to the illusion a moment more.

Let herself cling to Jacob.

Their bodies touched intimately at chest and thigh,

creating a warm cocoon that excluded the dawn chill. Her arms wrapped around his waist, their legs intertwined, and Isabella wasn't quite sure anymore where she left off and Jacob began.

Dangerous thoughts.

She stiffened and tried to pull away, but he tightened his arms and murmured into her hair, "No, stay."

His voice made the moment more real. Too real. Isabella froze, suddenly aware of her breasts pressed up against the hard wall of his chest, her arms clutching his torso.

Clinging.

But instead of pulling away, he held on tight and buried his face in her hair. "It's okay to be scared." He rocked her from side to side. "Being afraid doesn't make you like your mother. You're not her. Never were."

The words struck a chord, but she didn't want him to see, so she pushed away and wiped her eyes. "What did you see outside?"

He held her eyes a moment longer, as though he knew what she was thinking, what she was doing. But in the end, he blew out a breath and answered, "Not a thing. But he's out there."

She nodded. She felt it, too. A sense of watching eyes. Waiting violence.

Now was not the time for long conversations.

In silent accord, their recent whispered conversation buzzing between them like an unfinished sentence, they quickly packed the emergency kit and checked their weapons. Then they slipped from concealment and walked through the forest single-file.

Jacob broke the trail, using the compass feature of his watch to keep them heading nearly due west. Isabella followed, watching their back and moving branches now and then in an effort to obscure their tracks.

As she walked, she thought of their situation. Odds were that the black-clad man would catch up to them before they reached civilization. Wouldn't it be better to meet him on their terms? Thinking that, considering the implications, she sketched out a plan in her mind.

By the time they paused for a midmorning break, she had a strategy for turning the hunter into the hunted.

All she had to do was to convince Jacob to go along with it.

ON THE OTHER SIDE of the locked door, Hope heard the television babbling to itself in the cabin's common room, furry with static. She thought she caught references to Lunkinburg and a speech by Prince Nikolai.

She nearly closed her eyes on the stab of pain that accompanied the name. She remembered meeting the handsome freedom fighter, remembered talking to her husband late into the night about the king's despotic rule and the U.S. government's desire to see Nikolai on the throne.

She knew some people thought Louis had married her during a midlife crisis, casting her in the role of trophy wife though it was a first marriage for both of them. But that was far from the truth—it had been love, plain and simple. They had met at a charity dinner, each on the arm of someone different. A month later, he had called her for drinks. Six months after that, they had been married in a quiet ceremony and the twins had followed a discreet year later.

Now, holding their daughters close, she fought tears at the strength of her loneliness, at the fear that had driven her for the four days of their captivity.

Limping footsteps neared her door and paused. The door cracked open a notch and her heart spiked, as it always did when the men checked on her.

Through the partially open door, she heard Lyle say, "Another forty-eight hours and we're home free, right? We just turn the four of them over and head home?"

Fear iced Hope's heart at the confirmation that they weren't to be released when Louis arrived. Worse, the whole family was to be *turned over.* But to whom? And what would happen to them?

The door opened the rest of the way and Lyle stuck his angular face through. He glanced at Hope, then at each of the girls, his gaze seeming to linger longest on Tiff. His beady blue eyes sharpened and he licked his lips, but before Hope could screech at him to keep his filthy hands off her baby, Boone's voice called from the main room.

"They're not going anywhere. Get back over here and help me with this detonator."

Lyle pantomimed a kiss at Tiff, then shut and locked the door.

Hope steadied her breathing and looked down at her baby girls. They clung to her, silent and scared.

She forced a smile. "You guys ready to get out of

here? Remember, you're going to have to be quiet, no matter what happens. Okay?"

She waited until she got two identical nods before she set her daughters on the bed and lifted the mattress to uncover the flat piece of metal she'd managed to work free of the box spring. With it, she was able to pop out the last two screws, the ones she'd left in the frame in case the men checked.

Then she held her breath and eased the window up. It scraped and squeaked very faintly, then ran all the way to the top. Fresh air hit her like a warm slap, reminding her that they were far from Montana.

With her heart in her throat, she looped a bed sheet around Tiff's body, under her arms. She did the same for Becky, then lowered the girls to the ground outside, one at a time.

When Becky's face screwed up and tears threatened, Hope forced herself to smile and hold a finger to her lips before she whispered, "It'll be okay, sweetie. Mommy will be right there."

Please don't let her cry, Hope prayed. If either of the girls made a noise, it would be all over.

Heart thundering in her ears, so loud she couldn't even tell if the TV was still on, she eased through the window feet first, then kicked away from the building and dropped, landing safely away from her daughters.

Then she let out a breath. Okay. So far, so good.

Praying for strength, for luck, she lifted her daughters, propped one on each hip, and took a step away from the cabin.

And her luck ran out.

"Boone! She's out!" Lyle's shout came from behind her, from inside the house. A gun fired with a deep bellied roar and she screamed, expecting the burn of pain, but it didn't come.

She bolted forward, stumbled beneath the combined weight of her daughters and nearly fell.

"No!" She struggled to her feet with more will than strength and ran toward the trees, away from the parking area where Boone's men had parked two Jeeps and a pickup truck.

She had decided not to trust her luck that the keys might be in the vehicles. The woods seemed her best bet.

Two more shots boomed behind her, then Boone's voice shouted, "Stop shooting, you idiots! *Get her!*"

Boots thundered on the porch, and Hope put her head down and ran. The girls clung to her like silent limpets, little fingers digging into her shirt, into her skin. Into her heart.

She wanted to reassure them, but didn't have the breath. Instead she ran as fast as she could. She gained the treeline, but the sounds of pursuit neared.

She could do nothing more than clutch her babies tighter and run. She dodged trees and leaped a rotten log, her ankle turning when she landed. By force of will, she kept herself up and continued on.

Her mind cleared of every thought except one.

She had to escape. Had to get to Louis.

"Stop!" a voice shouted behind her. "Damn it, stop! We've planted—"

A shot cut off the words and was immediately followed by a ripping, crushing explosion. The forest floor blew up twenty feet ahead of Hope. The dirt and leaves leaped tree-high, and a wave of heat and concussion slapped her to her knees.

She stayed down as the flying dirt peppered her with moist chunks. Her mind reeled with shock and horror. Boone's men had booby trapped the forest around the cabin. She had nearly stepped on one of the traps.

Tiff buried her face in her mother's neck while Becky, the braver of the two, stared at the newly formed crater and opened her mouth on a piercing wail.

Dear God, Hope thought. *That could have been us.*

She heard footsteps crunch on the leaves behind her. She expected it to be Kane or one of her usual guards, and was surprised when Boone's voice said, "You should thank me for shooting the trip pad. If I hadn't, you and your daughters would be dead."

She bowed her head as Becky's wailing escalated, echoing all the fear and desperation Hope felt inside.

"Shut her up," Boone said calmly, "or I will."

The cold certainty in his voice was nearly as terrifying as the furious explosion or the three-foot-deep crater that gaped nearby.

"Hush, sweetie." Hope soothed Becky, then Tiff, as well, when the shier girl began to whimper. All the while, fine tremors ran through her and her heart thundered with what had almost happened.

Her heartbeat seemed to say, *Dead-dead, dead-dead, dead-dead.*

"Bring them," Boone snapped, and then his footsteps moved away. Rough hands grabbed Hope and wrestled the girls out of her arms.

"My babies!" Hope struggled as two men—she didn't know which ones and didn't care anymore—dragged her up from the ground and muscled her back to the cabin. "Please. Please!" she shouted, but wasn't even sure what she was begging for anymore.

Please give me my daughters back. Please don't hurt them. Please let us go.

Please let someone come for us.

But as she was hauled into the cabin and locked into a small, windowless room in the attic loft, it seemed that none of those prayers would be answered. They wouldn't let her see her daughters—she couldn't even hear them crying anymore! Though she begged and pleaded and screamed, Hope was left there, alone, until she curled up into a little ball and sobbed.

As she cried, that one last prayer echoed through her body alongside the fear.

Please let someone come for us.

Her mind cried, *Louis!* as though he might hear her and know of the danger he was walking into. But there was no reply.

Only emptiness.

DEEP IN THE scraggly woods, the hit man waited.

"There he is." Isabella gripped Jacob's forearm so hard he felt the imprint down to the bone.

Or maybe he was too sensitive to her touch. Too reactive to her, by far.

More likely, he thought with an internal grimace, it

was nerves from this crazy plan of hers. But damn it, what was their other option? It was either ambush the ambusher, or keep pushing on toward the road and hope he didn't catch up.

Jacob had agreed to Isabella's plan because he hadn't been able to come up with a better option, but he didn't like it. In fact, he was taking a breath to suggest they pack up and run for the road when she touched his arm and gestured toward a faint shadow of distant movement.

Dark clothes. A predator's gait. A drawn weapon.

She whispered, "You all set?"

He nodded and mouthed, *Let's do this.*

Without further conversation, they fanned the sulky embers of a small campfire and fed it slivers of wet wood. The resulting blaze was smoky enough to attract attention without being obvious.

He hoped.

When everything was set, when their pursuer dropped down into the slight ravine that bordered the site they'd chosen for their stand—he refused to think of it as a last stand—he turned to Isabella. She turned to him at the same moment and they locked eyes.

Contact arced between them. Connection.

Good luck, he mouthed, his mind half on the coming skirmish, half on the woman standing a breath away.

"You, too."

He didn't know which one of them moved first, whether he leaned down for her or she tipped up on her toes to reach for him. Maybe both.

He only knew that they met halfway.

Her lips were firm beneath his, strong, like Isabella herself. Then they parted, and he found the softness within, a striking contrast that lodged in his soul even as heat roared through his body, through his brain, and buffeted at his heart.

He crowded closer and felt her hands slide up and around his neck, felt the contrast of warm fall sunlight at his back, the molten heat of sex at his front. Felt the click of connection he hadn't realized he was missing until it buzzed through his body and cupped a warm hand around his heart.

The ground shifted beneath his feet and then righted, and he forced himself to release her and step back.

Without another word, though the tension snapped tight between them like an invisible silken cord, he said out loud, "You rest that arm. I'm going to have a look around."

He walked boldly into the trees, leaving Isabella to perch near the fire with her bandaged arm held close to her side.

He cursed the seconds that ticked by as he worked away from the campfire, then doubled back on it. This was the tricky part, the most dangerous part. She would be out of his sight for no more than a minute or two, and she held the 9 mm in the crook of her arm—which wasn't as badly injured as they wanted the hunter to believe.

It was stupid simple, but it was a plan. Make her appear weaker than she was. Make her seem isolated and vulnerable.

Use her as bait to draw the predator near.

Jacob heard a noise in the middle distance and cursed the heavy brush that obscured his view of Isabella, but they hadn't been able to find a better spot. Hadn't been willing to let this drag on another day when time was running out on their deadline.

Now he wondered whether this had been a good plan, after all.

Moments later he pushed through to a place where the brush opened up, and he saw Isabella. She sat near the smoky fire, arm in her lap, a worried frown on her face as she scanned the nearby woods and carefully didn't linger on the place where they had agreed he would hide.

Jacob let out a breath and a small measure of tension left him. Thank God. The bastard hadn't arrived yet.

Then a small noise came from behind him.

A cool gun muzzle pressed into the skin beneath his ear.

And a heavily accented voice said, "Nice try. But not good enough."

Chapter Twelve

Bodies crashed in the brush nearby and Isabella's heart froze when Jacob's voice shouted, "Isabella, run!"

She bolted to her feet, weapon at the ready, but all she could see was a pair of struggling figures, one dressed in denim, the other in black. She couldn't get a clean shot through the scrub.

Jacob had yelled for her to escape, but there was no way she was leaving without him, so she plunged into brush, cursing when it tore at her skin and clothing, slowing her down.

She burst into a small clearing and skidded to a halt. Tried for a clear shot.

The men grappled, feet slipping on leaves and dead branches as they wrestled for control of the black-clad man's gun.

Isabella's heart seized at the sight, then began to beat again in the heavy, deliberate rhythm she'd learned during her training.

There was no place for emotion here. This was her duty. The job she was trained for. Protection. Action and reaction. She had to block Jacob's face from her mind, block the strong line of his body and the memory of the conversations they'd shared over the past four days. The mind-blowing passion. The intimacy.

There was only the enemy. The target.

She squared her feet, lifted the 9 mm, and sighted. Jacob's face swung into view, and she froze.

This wasn't duty. This was Jacob.

He looked over and saw her, and his face twisted with irritation that she'd disobeyed his command, or maybe with disappointment that she was simply standing there, unable to move. Unable to fire.

What if she hit him? What then?

Insecurity, unusual and unacceptable, swamped her out of nowhere, paralyzing her finger on the trigger. Suddenly she was back in the Golf Resort, frozen by the blast of the stun grenade, unable to help her protectees.

Suddenly she was powerless.

The hunter, a dark-clad man with mid-brown hair, weathered skin and the cool eyes of a killer, followed Jacob's gaze and locked onto Isabella. A faintly satisfied smile touched his lips. He held Jacob off, turned and leveled his weapon directly at her.

Run! Isabella's brain screamed. *Duck!* But for all her training, she couldn't move, couldn't react.

"No!" Jacob chopped at the other man's arm, fouling his aim. As though it made no real difference to him which one of them died first, the killer fended off the attack and turned his weapon in a new direction.

Directly at Jacob.

Isabella saw the barrel align, saw the bastard's finger tighten on the trigger.

And her paralysis broke. She screamed, "No!" and fired convulsively.

Her shot caught the dark-clothed man high in the shoulder and spun him away from Jacob. Blood showed on his arm, a gleaming slick against the black cloth, but he didn't reach for the wound, didn't try to run.

Instead he kicked Jacob in the stomach, and when his opponent folded and dropped to his knees, the man in black turned on Isabella and fired.

And missed.

With a roar, Jacob lunged up and caught his enemy around the waist, sending them both tumbling to the forest floor. Not thinking now, only reacting, Isabella charged toward the struggling men, looking for an opening, for a gap to put a bullet, or maybe a well-placed kick.

The killer landed a heavy blow to Jacob's jaw and the combatants parted slightly, Jacob lurching away and the other man falling back to the ground.

Isabella's pulse pounded when she saw her chance. She stepped forward, set her foot on the man's injured shoulder, and bore down on the wound. When he groaned, stiffened and looked up at her, she pointed the 9 mm at his left eye. "Freeze."

But he didn't. He grabbed her ankle and yanked, bringing her down into the fight.

Even worse, when she hit the ground, she lost her grip on the 9 mm.

"Jacob!" she shouted, wincing when the enemy landed a blow on her injured arm. "Get his gun!"

Then the fight swept her up and Isabella was only conscious of sensory snippets. A fist flying past her nose to connect with Jacob's jaw. A blow to her mid-section and an arm across her throat. The smell of blood and the punishing pain of violence.

Then she was thrown away as though she weighed nothing. She hit the dirt hard, then spun back, searching for a weapon, for an opportunity to jump back into the fight.

But Jacob stood over their foe, holding the black-clad man's gun, keeping the bastard pinned to the ground.

The man spat something in a foreign tongue, his body tensed for action, for renewed battle.

"I said freeze," Jacob commanded in a low, cold voice. "Or I'll put another hole in you."

The man finally froze. He looked from Jacob to Isabella and back again. The tension drained from his body and a look of resignation crossed his weathered features.

He said something low and vicious, a curse maybe, or a prayer. Then he moved his jaws in a scissoring motion, and swallowed. Moments later his body jerked, bowed upward and he let out a strangled cry.

And died.

Damn! He must have had a suicide capsule! Isabella lurched forward, brain jammed with horror that he'd taken his own life rather than be questioned. Anger for the same reason. Disgust at the cowardice, frustration at what it meant to their quest to save Cooper's family.

And over it all, basic human distress that she'd watched a man die.

But when she reached down, hands shaking slightly, Jacob's arms caught her and held her fast. "It's no use. He's gone." Then he held her away from him and scanned her from head to toe. "Are you okay?"

"Fine." She nodded automatically, without bothering to check. "You?"

"Fine." But he didn't look away, didn't let her go. His eyes were dark pools of tension and his fingers brought a fine tremor of electricity to her skin. "Why didn't you run when I told you?"

"Because I wasn't going to leave you behind." The words arrowed through her even as she spoke them, taking on a life beyond the immediate situation.

He looked as though he wanted to argue, as though he wanted to yell at her, to shake her for being who she was. Or maybe that was something else she saw in his eyes, something wild and wicked and hot, close to anger but not quite. She wasn't sure of her own emotions anymore, how could she possibly interpret his?

But instead of shouting, or shaking her, or even turning on his heel and walking away for a moment alone to marshal his temper, he surprised her by grimacing and nodding. "Yeah. I know the feeling."

Then he surprised her again by pulling her into his arms and kissing her. Hard.

This was no halfway meeting of give-and-take as their earlier kisses had been. This was all him. All heat and lightning and power.

Then she stepped into his embrace and opened her mouth to join him, and it wasn't about him anymore.

It was *them*.

The heat they generated together was flash and flame, friction and chafe, hotter than she remembered from before, but somehow less frightening for the intensity. It was as though time and experience had given her perspective, or maybe she'd grown into herself.

This wasn't about her being needy, wasn't about her being her mother. It was about her being herself.

It was about her wanting Jacob. Being wanted in return.

They strained together, flesh pressing against flesh through ragged clothing and the bumps and bruises of the past few days. They twined together, tasting and claiming, with no thought of a nip or a tease. There was only heat.

And want.

And adrenaline.

On the last thought, Isabella stiffened and pulled away just as Jacob did the same. Their eyes dropped synchronously to the forest floor. To the corpse of the man in black.

The mutual message was clear. This was neither the time nor the place.

But even as she acknowledged it, defeat echoed hollowly within Isabella, beating back the heat. Disappointment thumped alongside her heart.

There would never be a time and place for Jacob and her. Or maybe there had been, for a few months during their senior year of college.

"Hey." His soft word brought her head up. He touched a finger to her cheek, traced a long, gentle stroke down the side of her face. "We'll talk, after. I promise."

He looked as though he wanted to say more, wanted to let her down gently this time instead of simply disappearing. But instead he let his hand fall away and turned his attention to the body.

Isabella forced herself to do the same. She knelt and tried not to remember the agony etched in the man's face as he died. Tried not to think that she'd seen him take his own life rather than be questioned or dishonored.

What sort of loyalty could demand such a sacrifice?

Knowing the answer even before she asked, Isabella said, "This isn't one of your militiamen, is it?"

Jacob shook his head. Then he bent, retrieved the weapons from the forest floor and checked them over before handing her the 9 mm. "No. He's not one of the escaped fugitives, and I'd bet money he's not a member of the MMFAFA."

"Because he spoke a foreign language, and the militiamen are known xenophobes," she said.

"Yeah." He turned away and headed back toward the clearing where their fire continued to produce fitful smoke. "And because he was too well supplied. Boone loads his people with weapons and explosives, but not the high-tech stuff. Not night vision, gas masks and choppers. At least, he never did before."

Someone else was in charge. But who?

Isabella followed Jacob to the clearing and helped him repack their diminished emergency kit. The medical supplies were low and the canteens were nearly empty. They had enough ration bars to last them some time, but she'd kill for a cheeseburger.

Jacob zipped the pack and hefted it. "Let's cover the body with a quick cairn and leave a marker, so there's something left for the authorities to find when we send them back."

It took them nearly a backbreaking hour to cover the body with rocks large enough to foil all but the most determined scavengers. It took another half hour for them to work their way free of the forest and out to the long, rocky incline that led to a low range of hills they would have to cross to pick up the road.

Isabella's legs ached at the thought. The grade was shallow, but it was a long way up.

"Come on." Jacob held out a hand. "The sooner we start, the sooner it's over."

"Good point." She took his hand and let him tug her up onto the rocky slope. He didn't let go immediately, but kept the contact and the gentle pressure that pulled her onward.

And instead of pushing away, she curled her fingers into his.

For now, she'd take the strength where she could find it.

JACOB LED ISABELLA through the day and into the evening, pausing for only brief breaks and to fill the canteens at a cold river they then slogged across.

He called a halt as the purple of dusk crept to midnight-blue. Isabella would never admit it, but he knew she was all done. Though she still walked with long, sure strides, her body had tightened in on itself, and her lips were pressed together as though holding moans inside, or maybe curses.

Jacob held back the same curses as he waved her to a low rocky outcropping that would provide them some small shelter. He hated to push her, hated to see her push herself, but there was no better option.

They had to get to civilization as quickly as possible. Time was running out. And though the corpse had yielded few clues and there had been no sign of the dark helicopter, he felt the danger closing in.

Though he didn't yet understand how the enemy had learned of his and Isabella's plans, they had to know the ultimate destination. Hangman's cabin.

All they needed to do was to set a trap.

Or had they already done so? Was this entire cross country chase one big setup?

Hell, he didn't know anymore. He didn't know anything anymore.

Isabella collapsed to the ground and leaned back against the rocky backdrop. "I'll take a watch. You need to rest." Her words were slurred with fatigue, but her eyes dared him to mention it, dared him to treat her as weak.

Hell, she was anything but. She was an incredibly strong woman who'd reached the end of her endurance.

Knowing it, and feeling an odd punch of pride, Jacob dropped down beside her, so they touched at hip and shoulder, both facing back the way they had come.

"We both need to rest," he said after a moment. "We'll take turns."

She nodded and he felt her shiver against him. Suddenly conscious of the cold, wet material of his pants against his legs, he pushed to his feet. "I'll get a fire going." When she protested, he held up a hand. "We can't afford not to. We're higher up—the night's going to get chilly."

It did. It got cool, then downright cold. It got lonely, once Jacob's only company was Isabella pressed against him, dead to the world, and the fitful crackle of the fire that provided more light than warmth as the night wore on.

Just after dawn, when his body finally gave out and dropped him toward oblivion, Jacob felt Isabella turn in his arms and nestle up against him.

And then he heard the helicopter.

Approaching fast.

"Iz! WAKE UP! We've gotta move!"

Jacob's urgent voice pierced her dreams and brought her up through the foggy layers to consciousness.

Then she heard the rotors, and the last dregs of sleep vanished. She bolted to her feet and fought the dizziness of quick movement as she joined Jacob in stomping out the last of the fire.

He cursed. "If they've got infrared, they'll see the embers." He held out a hand. "Come on, let's get out of here!"

Her heart thundered in dread, but she didn't bother to tell him that they could never outrun a helicopter, that they would be better off hiding, hoping a thicket of trees or a rock niche would obscure their body heat.

She didn't bother, because the sluggish dawn light

showed what she'd been too tired to notice the night before. They were on the ridge apex. There were few trees and the only rocks nearby were the ones that had formed their scant overnight shelter.

There was nothing big enough to shield them from visual detection, never mind more sensitive scans. So she checked that the 9 mm was secure in her pocket, and grabbed his hand. "Let's go."

But he remained still, head cocked, as the helicopter came near.

Fear screamed through her and she tugged at him. "Jacob? Let's go!"

"No, wait." He held up his free hand. "I recognize that engine."

Every cell of her body screamed for flight, for hiding, as the sound grew ever louder. But she trusted Jacob, she told herself. He was a pilot. He knew his engines.

She hoped.

Then it was too late for hope, too late for flight. Lights crested the ridge and speared down toward them.

Jacob lifted a hand at the aircraft and in the fitful light of dawn, Isabella could just make out the lettering on the side of the red and white chopper.

BSBH. *Big Sky Bounty Hunters.*

It wasn't until the helicopter touched down, the door opened and Cameron Murphy swung out, relief written plainly on his handsome features, that she let herself believe.

They'd been rescued. Even better, it was Sunday morning.

Next stop, Devil Mountain.

Chapter Thirteen

In reality, between fuel stops, a quick E.R. visit to get Isabella some antibiotics for her arm, and debriefing, it took them most of the day to get to Devil Mountain. More specifically, to a small motel in the next town over, which the bounty hunters had rented for use as a command post as they planned the next day's raid.

But Isabella would think about that later. At the moment her priority was a shower. A long, hot one. The sort of shower that would blast away the past few days, that could ease the aches and pains, wash away the memory of a stranger killing himself with one crunch on a drug-filled, hollowed-out tooth, like something out of a Cold-War-era spy movie.

She shivered, the memory seeming somehow more terrifying now that they had been rescued by the bounty hunters, who had refused to believe the FAA's report of "no survivors." Once the bloodhounds had picked up a trail leading away from the downed jet, Cameron had made an educated guess of Jacob's track, and the men had started working a search grid with binoculars during the day and infrared scanners at night.

Isabella could have wept with relief at their rescue. Since then, she'd been tempted to scream with frustration and confusion as Jacob seemed to distance himself more with each passing moment.

She told herself she should be grateful, that his behavior would make it easier to say goodbye.

But it wasn't working as she stared into the mirror at her own bruised face and tried to be completely, brutally honest with herself.

It was true that her spontaneous combustion at the crash site could be blamed on adrenaline and a survivor's rush. But something had happened between them while they were stranded out in that wilderness. They had made a connection. Found forgiveness for each other. For themselves.

So what was she going to do about it?

"Nothing," she said very clearly into the mirror. "You're going to do nothing about Jacob Powell, because he isn't your focus. Hope, Becky and Tiff are your focus right now. They're your duty."

With that in mind, she showered quickly when she wanted to linger, and pulled on newly bought clothes with little thought to how they fit or looked. She dragged a cheap brush through her still-wet hair and left the plain room without a backward glance.

She paused at the door to a small suite three rooms away, and knocked. Without waiting for an answer, she pushed through and was unsurprised to find Jacob there, along with the eight bounty hunters Cameron had selected for the raid.

They had already discussed and discarded the idea of

calling in the authorities. For one, it would take too much convincing and they didn't have the time to spare. For another, they were unsure of Cooper's place in all this.

The Secretary of Defense had refused to call in the authorities when conventional hostage wisdom said otherwise. He'd had her discredited with the Service almost immediately, blocking her from providing any help at all. And he'd changed his position on the Lunkinburg controversy right after the abduction.

Was he being held up for political reasons? Or was something more sinister going on? Something more devious?

It was entirely possible that this whole thing had been a setup. That he'd known she had planted the bug and had sent the killers after her. But it was equally possible that Cooper was as much a pawn in this game as she was. That he was trying only to keep his family safe.

They wouldn't know which until the next day, when they raided the cabin up on Devil Mountain.

Hating the unanswered questions and the potential dangers, she sat on a spongy couch at the opposite end from where Jacob's weight pressed the cushions down, creating a tilt that threatened to pull her nearer his warmth. She ignored him, ignored the questions that still swirled between them, and fixed her attention on Cameron. "What's the plan?"

But it was Jacob who turned to her and answered, "We go in just after dawn."

THEY TWEAKED the plan for nearly two hours while Jacob tried to stifle his restlessness. Cameron ordered

in pizza somewhere in the middle of an argument between Mike Clark and Tony Lombardi over the results
of their early surveillance, which had revealed no sign
of the woman or children, and only a cursory guard ro-
tation made up of two men—identified as Kane Myers
and Lyle Nelson, two of Boone's goons.

"It doesn't add up," Mike insisted, leaning forward
and gesturing with a can of soda—no drinking before
the raid—to make his point. "Boone Fowler isn't stupid, and his men have good survival skills. Even if
they're getting outside help from King Aleksandr—and
I still say that's a big *if*—I don't see Boone being this
lax. And then there's the stance and attitude of the
guards. It's not quite right."

Jacob's attention shifted away from the warmth radiating from Isabella, who sat nearby on the small-feel-
ing couch and focused on Mike. "What do you mean?"

The body-language expert shrugged. "They're vigi-
lant, sure. But they're not paying as much attention to
the nearby woods as they should be. They seem…too
casual."

Jacob shifted in his seat, hyper-aware of Isabella, of
the dark circles beneath her mossy-green eyes and the
bruise shadows that marred her fine skin. Frustrated by
his continued attention split, he frowned. "What do you
think is going on? Do you think this is a setup? That the
hostages aren't even in there?"

That was one explanation for why there had been no
sign of the woman or children. Another was that they
were being held somewhere out of surveillance range.

The third possibility—that they had already been killed—wasn't one he wanted to consider.

But Mike shook his head. "I don't know about that. But Boone's men are too cocky. I think they've got another layer of defense, one that we haven't seen yet."

The suggestion hung on the air like a menace until Cameron broke the silence with a quiet curse and two damning words. "Booby traps."

At Isabella's questioning look, Jacob elaborated, "The MMFAFA, and particularly two of the fugitives—Marcus Smith and Leroy Edwards—are fond of explosives. Trip wires. Man traps. That sort of thing."

She nodded. "Which leaves us where?"

"Proceeding very, very carefully," Jacob answered.

After that, Cameron closed the meeting with a brief pep talk and an order for everyone to get a good night's rest and meet back at the suite at 4:00 a.m.

They had decided to go in the next morning, which would give them the best opportunity to scout the hidden mines. Unfortunately it would leave them exposed once they left the safety of the forest near the cabin.

It was a calculated risk. Hopefully it would pay off.

The bounty hunters mumbled good-nights to each other and to Isabella. Some would sleep. Others would lie awake and plan.

Jacob feared he would fall into the latter category, especially after he watched her walk down the motel row to her room, step inside and close the door without looking back.

He wanted to go after her but didn't know how. The brash young man he'd been in college would have knocked on her door and charmed his way in, or maybe challenged her to a game of darts.

But the man he'd become, who remembered the taste of her on his lips and the feeling of her coming apart in his arms after little more than a kiss, couldn't bring himself to walk down the narrow cement strip to her door, couldn't bring himself to knock or to speak with her once she opened the door.

Because what could he say? What had happened between them in those woods? He wasn't even sure anymore. The whole experience felt like a dream, like a handful of days outside of reality.

They were back in the real world now, poised to move against Boone and his men the next day. Isabella had insisted on going in with the first wave, because Hope and the girls knew her and because she had a score to settle. Cameron had agreed. Jacob had been outvoted. Concern for her gelled in a nasty ball in his gut, even as part of him tried to look beyond the raid to the future.

If they managed to get through Boone's booby traps and breach the cabin, *if* they succeeded in—God willing—finding and releasing the hostages, and *if* they got out unharmed…what then?

Isabella lived and worked in D.C., which wasn't an option for him. Even if he could bring himself to move back into his parents' world, he didn't want to leave Montana. He'd found a piece of himself there and didn't want to let it go.

And if they could make it work, did he want it to? The single life was comfortable for him. No bumps, no bruises. The only complications he faced on a daily basis were work-related, and he had the other bounty hunters for backup when he needed them.

A relationship, on the other hand, was one-on-one. Man and woman. Two people against the world, and sometimes against each other.

The prospect shouldn't have been tempting.

But because it was, and because he didn't know how to squelch the sense of impending doom, didn't know whether it was attached to the next day's raid or the prospect of Isabella going back to D.C. when it was over, he turned and stalked to his own room.

He banged the door shut, and told himself the gunshot-loud slam was a statement. He wouldn't be going to her. Wouldn't complicate an already complicated situation, no matter how much his body begged for hot release, how much his soul yearned for soft comfort.

He showered quickly, trying to scrub away the images of the past few days. Trying to eradicate the memory of the paralyzing fear he'd felt when she'd jumped into the fight with the man in black…trying to wash off her essence, which seemed to cling to him now, like the smell of female flesh.

The smell of sex.

His first winter in Montana, he'd laughed with the other men at the sight of a bull moose in full rut. The poor sod had run around half-stiff all the time, worrying at his small herd of females for the duration of mating season.

These days, Jacob understood how he felt. Since Isabella had marched back into his life, he'd existed in a state of half-terror, half-arousal. He didn't like it. Couldn't handle it.

So he'd get her through the next day and do his damnedest to make sure she survived the raid unscathed. And then he'd put her on a plane back to the east coast and out of his life.

At the resolve, he felt a measure of relief, a measure of sadness. But he was convinced it was the right answer, the only answer.

Then he looped the towel across his hips and padded through the empty motel room, past the empty bed, and parted the heavy, light-blocking blinds, not even knowing why until he saw her sitting alone on a picnic bench in a clearing behind the motel.

She sat on the tabletop, her knees drawn up to her chest to conserve warmth, or maybe to provide a shield from the darkness of the forest beyond. A single spotlight illuminated her with light that should have been harsh but instead softened the gleam of her auburn hair and made her seem smaller. Less intimidating, though he'd never been quite sure how he could be intimidated by such a petite woman.

Fear had more to do with emotion than with size when it came to her.

He stayed still, watching her. Though his brain had listed all the reasons he should stay away, he wanted to go to her, to hold her and protect her from whatever lay in the darkness beyond the light. He wanted to wrap himself around her and pull her inside his heart the way he remembered doing years before.

The sane, rational part of him said to shut the

blinds and back away. Go to bed and sleep through the night—or stare at the ceiling if that was what it took. He didn't need this, didn't need her, because he liked the life he'd made himself. He was a free agent, his own controller. He didn't want to give anyone else a vote.

But those thoughts were drowned out by the sight of the curve of her cheek, so he stood still and watched.

Then, as if she knew he was there, knew he'd been watching, she turned and looked at him over her shoulder. She didn't wave, didn't gesture, and after a long moment, she turned back to the dark forest as though dismissing him.

Or maybe inviting him.

SHE SENSED HIM before she heard his approach. Or maybe that was wishful thinking, her desire for a connection that wasn't meant to be. It was such thoughts running through her head that had sent her outdoors into the cool California night.

As though he'd read her mind, Jacob draped a jacket across her shoulders before climbing up to sit beside her, his feet on the bench below, his hands linked loosely between his knees.

She expected that at least a few of the bounty hunters were awake and pacing, and imagined that they paused by their windows to watch the scene on the picnic bench outside. But she didn't feel their stares as she pulled the jacket tighter across her chest and tried not to inhale the masculine scent that rose up from it. Instead she felt cocooned by the night, held together with

Jacob in a small, breathless space that contained the two of them and nothing more.

Perhaps feeling the same thing, or perhaps not caring either way, Jacob spoke normally, his voice seeming loud in the night. "We should talk."

"No." She reached out and touched his linked hands, and felt a shiver of surprise at the warmth, at the fact that she'd touched him at all. "Let's not bother. We've said what's needed to be said. You're sorry about being such a jerk in college, and I've realized it was never about me being like my mother. It was about both of us needing to grow up."

"We're grown up now," he said, the words emerging almost reluctantly from his mouth. He looked at her and his eyes were too close. Too unreadable.

She leaned away just a fraction, but enough to feel the cool air move between them, forming an insubstantial barrier. "Yes, we are," she agreed. "Regardless of what happened at the crash site, we've grown up and apart."

The air seemed to still, waiting for him to deny it, to tell her there was a chance for them, even though she knew there wasn't.

"I'd say it's more that we grew up in parallel," he said.

Tension hummed between then, unwanted, unacknowledged. It burned beneath her skin with the insistent tempo of her heartbeat, and seemed to say. *To-night…to-night…to-night.*

After tonight, they would be headed in separate directions, one way or another.

She let go of his hand and wrapped her arms around her knees once again, shutting the cold out. Her heart bounded in her chest, but she forced the words as though they were casual. "You owe me a future claim from our dart game in D.C."

His body stiffened, his eyes sharpened on her and he swallowed almost convulsively. "Yeah."

The single word sounded as though it had been pushed from his chest by force of will. By passion.

She wet her lips and damned the butterflies in her stomach, the tingle of fear in her fingertips. Not fear of him, or fear of what was to come the next day, but fear of that precise moment.

Fear of rejection.

"Tell me..." She swallowed and tried again. "Tell me what you want. Tell me the truth. What you really, really want."

His eyes narrowed, as though he hadn't expected the question, as though he'd expected her to ask for the physical and instead she'd demanded something more difficult.

More emotional.

He looked at her for a long moment before responding. Then the tension drained from his body, from the air between them, and the heat in his eyes was banked behind cool green shadows.

"I want you to stay safe tomorrow. I want to find Cooper's wife and children alive, and I want Boone and his men captured." He took a breath, held it for a moment, then let it out. "I want justice, and then I want to get back to my life."

Meaning that he wanted her out of it.

Trying to tell herself she was relieved, Isabella exhaled, uncurled herself and dropped down from the picnic table. "Good. We're on the same page, then." She thought about giving the jacket back, but didn't relish losing the warmth, so she kept it as she turned for the motel.

Jacob reached out a hand and turned her to face him. "Isabella…"

She backed away. "It's okay. I understand."

And she did. She understood that for all the time she'd spent learning to control her emotions, to school herself to strength, he was still tougher than she, still able to walk away from what he wanted to protect himself from caring too much.

From giving up control.

Damn him.

She felt the press of tears, felt the scream build in her soul, and knew she needed to get away, fast, and retreat with her dignity intact. So she turned and headed back for the motel, not turning when he called her name, not turning when she heard his muttered curse.

Not even turning when she didn't hear his footsteps following behind.

She set her jaw and walked around to the front of the motel. She nodded at Cameron, who sat outside his room with a cell phone to his ear, making soft, meaningful noises to his wife, or maybe his child.

The tears pressed harder, but she held them in until she gained her room.

She, at least, would have her breakdown in private.

But once she was inside the motel room, the urge to

cry vanished, leaving only leaden disappointment behind, shored up by a wash of anger.

Damn him. Even after all these years, he was still a coward. For all his physical presence and strength, he'd been too chicken to tell her the truth and to break it off cleanly back in college, and he was too afraid to chance things now, even for a night.

Angry now, she fisted her hands and spun back toward the door.

It swung open without warning. Jacob stood framed in the doorway, shoulders nearly touching the trim, his face set in a scowl.

Her heart thundered with anticipation, with dread, but she kept her feet planted and lifted her chin defiantly. "Well?"

He stepped inside and kicked the door shut. Before she even registered that he'd moved, he crossed the room and pulled her into his arms. Without a word, without an explanation, without warning of any kind besides the flare of heat between them, he kissed her.

It was a branding, a possession, a bold statement of need that recalled the flash and the flame of them coming together beside the wrecked jet, when she'd ignited to his touch and lost her soul.

Minutes later, or maybe longer, he pulled away, breathing as ragged as hers, and said, "I lied. When you asked what I wanted, I lied."

She dug her fingers into his forearms, as much to keep herself on her feet as to hold him close. "I know."

His eyes were clear green as they searched hers, looking for answers she didn't have. "I like my life."

"Me, too," she managed to say, though she had to force the words through a tremble that spoke of her own lie. "So we keep it casual. One night between friends. The mutual release we didn't get back in the desert." She looked away so he couldn't see the flinch in her eyes when she said, "The goodbye we never got to have."

When she glanced back at him, she saw that he wanted to protest, to argue, even to pull back and leave. But her body wouldn't allow it, not now. Her heart wouldn't allow it, though he'd never know that she'd done the unthinkable, the inexplicable, and fallen for him all over again, even knowing there was no hope of a future between them.

Knowing that, and knowing it was her problem, not his, she raised a finger to his lips before he could speak and deny the moment. "Don't overthink it, Jacob. Let's just go with the flow."

The words resonated in her head, in her soul, and she realized he'd said something similar to her when they'd first met, when she'd wanted to pull back because they'd just met and the feelings between them seemed too huge to manage.

His eyes sparked with the same memory, wiping away the moment of hesitation. This time when he reached for her, he meant business.

She went willingly, almost greedily, into his arms. This was her choice. His choice. They could have tonight and then move on, move away, have the closure she had lacked all these years.

If not for the lack of closure, why had she fallen

back under his sensual spell so easily? It wasn't weakness, she told herself, wasn't destiny or any of those rose-colored words she'd used to describe them so long ago. It was chemistry.

And if she brought her emotions along for the ride, that was her problem. Not his. Not theirs.

She poured herself into the kiss, into his arms, and reveled in the heat that blasted, binding them, searing them until she wasn't sure where her skin ended and his began.

There was only sizzle and smoke and the pressure of perfection in her chest.

She twisted her fingers in his shirt and became aware of the cool dampness of the material, the cold slickness of his hair and the clean smell that said he'd showered before coming outside to sit with her in the crisp night air. She curled around him, stroking, inciting, trying to bring warmth where there was chill, heat where there was cool.

He groaned into her mouth and caught her hands in his, stilling them, making her slow down. She felt the fine tremors race through his too tight muscles and knew he fought for the one thing he valued above all else.

Control.

But this night wasn't about control, it was about the loss of it, about giving in to the physical storm that had raged between them since that first moment in the Big Sky cabin, when the crowd of men had parted to let him through and their eyes had met after so long and they both realized that the heat between them had survived thirteen years.

Worse, it had intensified.

Now, she rode that heat, let it pour through her, consume her from within. She left her hands in his, knowing she didn't need them to incite, to inflame. She leaned in and nipped his lower lip, then soothed that place with her tongue.

His body stiffened against her. His breath caught.

Emboldened, she crowded him, bumping against his body and challenging him to take a step, either forward or back.

But he did neither. He stood fast. She felt his control break with a nearly audible snap, and she felt a flush of victory. Of excitement.

Love me! she wanted to say, but instead tilted her head toward the motel bed. "Any interest?"

Humor flared beside the heat in his expression. "Oh, yeah. I'm interested."

With that, he scooped her up off the floor and carried her to the bed. Not in a romantic carrying-the-bride-over-the-threshold manner, but in a total he-man toss over one shoulder, then a bounce onto the bed.

Isabella's heart pounded with lust, with joy. She stifled the giggle when she landed on the bed, but let free with the approving murmur when he shucked the damp shirt off over his head and joined her. The mattress gave beneath his weight, rolling them tight together.

She didn't compare his broad, muscular shoulders to that of the young man she had known, and she didn't assume she knew what the man liked because she'd known the boy. In that first instant of them being pressed together from chest to toe, she found those memories, those comparisons, gone. In that moment, she was a woman and he a man, and it was as though they were coming together for the first time.

And the last.

She shoved aside the desperation brought by the thought, shoved aside any thought at all, and threw herself into the moment, into each sensation and spark.

The future would wait, damn it.

She reached for the hem of her new shirt and found his fingers there before hers. He eased the shirt up and over her head, and hissed his approval at the bare skin beneath, unfettered by the bra she'd left off after her shower.

He pulled back, and she felt his eyes on her bare skin like a touch. Though she was fit, and proud of it, Isabella felt a momentary flash of shyness, of nerves.

His eyes darkened, then rose to meet hers. His expression turned serious, and he parted his lips to speak.

"Hush." She reached up to kiss him, to stem the words one of them might regret. "We've already said what needs to be said."

"No." He touched his lips to her forehead with gentle, utterly uncharacteristic sweetness. "I haven't yet told you that you're beautiful."

The words shimmered through her like light, though she struggled not to let them matter. Instead she smiled and said, "You grew up good, too."

She reached up and kissed him again, urging him to drop down beside her, atop her, and move beyond speaking, because she feared if they talked more, she would lose her nerve.

Or her heart.

But as she slid back into his kiss, into his arms, the word *beautiful* slipped through her consciousness and into her soul. It shouldn't have mattered that he thought her pretty, but it did.

The word sang within the whirl of heat that rose up to consume her and flow into him. They strained together, her breasts flattened against his chest, their hands seeking to hold rather than stroke, bind rather than incite.

A sense of wholeness rolled through Isabella, frightening in its intensity. She needed to shift gears, to get them away from slow touches and words like *beautiful* and push the interlude back to flash and flame, to safe words like lust and chemistry.

This was about sex, not making love. It had to be.

But when she dug her fingers into the solid cords of muscle in his back and scissored her legs over his hips, urging him to hurry, to take…he didn't hurry, didn't take. Instead he rained soft kisses on her face, along the too sensitive column of her throat, urging her to come along for the ride.

For a man whose control had snapped, he had exquisite restraint now, touching, tasting, murmuring meaningless endearments that glowed in her soul. But when she opened her eyes and looked at him, really looked at him, she saw the wildness in his eyes that told her he wasn't in control at all.

He was being controlled by something beyond the chemistry, beyond the heat and lust.

And for once, he wasn't fighting it.

She stared into his eyes, into the heart he so rarely listened to, and when he brought his hands up to frame her face, when he touched his lips to hers almost questioningly, as though he didn't know what was happening between them any more than she did, she felt her resistance snap and disappear.

This was real. *She* was real, as were her emotions. Maybe they were only real for this one perfect moment in time, but it would be enough.

She would make it be enough.

Moving more slowly, in less of a hurry now, they stripped each other bare and came together once again, skin to skin, limbs twined around limbs.

The pressure of it, the beauty of it, built in Isabella's heart until she feared she might burst and float away. His touch kept her grounded, then sent her spinning, twirling into the heat that built slowly at first, then to a ferocious crescendo.

It was on the crest of that fiery wave that he came to her, thrust into her on a shout and a prayer that echoed in her soul. They fit together, strained together to reach the first pinnacle almost effortlessly, with little dimming of the pressure or the want.

They climbed the next wave together, building joyously to an explosive release that coiled tight in Isabella's center, in her heart and mind, until it blasted outward, radiating through her limbs and soul until she screamed with it.

The sound was echoed in his shout. Four syllables.

Her name.

THEY LAY TOGETHER afterward, breathing hard. Isabella felt her heart beat slowly, heard his do the same where it echoed beneath her ear as she lay across his chest.

She felt drained of the tension that had driven her for so long. In the place of that tension, she felt a warm safety, a glow of contentment. Of completion.

With it came a spurt of fear, though the emotion felt distant, blunted by the arms that held her, the feel of the man beneath her. But even blunted, the fear was powerful, as was the knowledge.

She had turned to him for sex. But she had ended up making love.

His heart steadied beneath her cheek, his hands slid along her spine, soothing, inciting, then falling away as his breathing deepened and he eased toward sleep on a single, four-syllable word.

Isabella.

She should get up, she told herself, get out. She should take a walk and clear her head.

But even as her brain told her that was silly, that was running away, she felt her own limbs grow heavy, felt sleep reach up to claim her, to pull her down into the thick, snuggly warmth they had created together.

Just one minute, she told herself. *Just a quick nap.*

And she slept.

Too long.

The next thing she knew, the alarm was buzzing and everything was motion. Chaos. She woke, befuddled when the yielding surface beneath her surged and cursed. Before she'd even realized she was still sleeping atop Jacob, he had rolled her to the side and lunged from the bed, wild-eyed.

He stood in the center of the room, chest heaving, staring at her as though he'd never seen her before, or maybe he'd never seen her that way before.

He rubbed quick hands across his face, then looked to their tangled clothes. "Well."

Isabella's heart stuttered at the confusion in his expression, the dismay. She gritted her teeth and banished the disappointment. What had she expected? They had agreed, after all. One night, no complications.

Well, the night was over. But the complications had just begun.

She heard Cameron's voice outside, calling for the others, felt the hum of activity in the adjoining rooms, and knew they would be hard-pressed to disguise the fact that Jacob had spent the night with her.

They were consenting adults, it was true, but they were also riding into battle together. Complications had no place on this raid.

So she nodded toward the back window. "You could sneak out. Nobody needs to know."

Something flashed in Jacob's eyes. Irritation, maybe, or temptation. He flattened his lips together and reached for his clothing, shaking it free of hers. "No." He said the word with his back to her as he pulled on his briefs and jeans. "We go out the front door. Together. Cameron will just have to deal."

Minutes later, dressed and ready to go, Isabella couldn't stop the flush from climbing her cheeks when Jacob opened the motel door and gestured her through, then followed at her back. Seven bounty hunters stood in the parking area near the vehicles, armed and ready for war.

Seven pairs of eyes fixed on her, then Jacob. Seven pairs of eyebrows lowered, as though each man was making his own calculation of what this might mean, how it might confuse the raid.

A small part of Isabella wished they would tell her when they figured it out.

Then Cameron swung out of the main suite and jerked his head at the vehicles. "Come on. Let's go get Cooper's family."

Chapter Fourteen

It was just beginning to lighten inside the small attic room when Hope heard the noise.

She'd spent the past day or so in an angry, drugged haze. They'd taken her babies away. She hadn't heard them in days, not even a cry.

What if they were dead?

On the thought, her mind sent her sliding back into that warm, gray fuzz.

Then she heard the noise again. It sounded like an owl's hoot, but not like any owl she'd heard since she'd been here. She started to shrug it off, to slip back into that beckoning grayness, but a sliver of consciousness pricked at her.

Something was different. But what?

She forced her eyes open, heaved herself to the side of the narrow bed and noticed one difference right away. She was vertical. Her mind—such as it was—started to clear.

They must've missed a dose of whatever they'd been pumping into her system.

A spark of life, of fear, worked its way through her and she stood, swaying. She stumbled to the door and pressed her ear to the cheap wood.

Silence.

In the week she'd been held in the cabin, both before her escape attempt and after, she'd never heard silence in the cabin. Even in the deepest depths of night, there had always been a sense of movement, of guards walking the porch or sitting in a downstairs room and passing the hours over cards and lies.

She pressed closer to the door and the noise came again. Only this time, she recognized it. It wasn't an owl. It was one of her daughters, making the sort of cooing noise both girls had outgrown at about a year. The noise that said they were waking up.

Anger suffused her, along with near-paralytic relief. The girls had been drugged, too! They were alive, and from the sounds of it, being held in the room next door.

Adrenaline and rage flooded her, driving away most of the drugged lethargy and giving her strength to stand. To plan.

She heard footsteps in the hallway outside her door and froze. A second set of steps moved to join the first, only these footsteps dragged and bumped with a noticeable limp. Lyle.

The gravelly voice confirmed it when he said, "Sounds like the brats are waking up. Should we check on them?"

Her whole body stiffened, and her mind screamed, *Don't you dare touch my babies!* But the other voice— it sounded like Kane—said, "Nah. Cooper'll be here soon. Let him deal with them for as long as necessary."

Dread knotted in Hope's stomach alongside failure. She should have escaped and warned him. Now he would be trapped alongside them. *Handed over,* as Boone had said.

"What about the wife?" Kane's voice asked.

"Leave her. She'll come to over the next hour or so, but she won't cause any trouble. We can check on her later."

The footsteps moved off down the hall, one set measured, the other set ragged. Hope strained close to the door, but didn't hear another set of steps or voices. She couldn't be certain, but it sounded as though Lyle and Kane were the only men left in the cabin.

Which meant that Boone and the others were gone. But where?

Had they left for good? Or were they even now ranged around the cabin among the traps? Waiting.

Watching.

Hope's heart thundered in her ears. She needed to do something. She needed to escape, to get her girls out of here. If she met Louis halfway, maybe they could get free. Maybe they would all survive.

Maybe.

Pulse racing, palms sweating from a combination of fear and her body's desire to clear the last remnants of the drug from her system, she sat on the bed. Through the wall, she heard a second coo join the first as her other daughter woke up.

She felt tears well, felt possibilities argue with despair, and pressed her hand against the wall.

"Don't worry, babies," she whispered, not loud

enough to carry, "Mommy's here. I'll take care of you. I promise."

Then she snuffled back the tears and pushed herself to her feet once again. It was time to make a plan. Lyle had said he'd check on her in an hour.

Well, this time she'd be waiting for him.

"IT'S WAY TOO QUIET," Mike reported from his forward station near the cabin. The tiny radio buzzed in Jacob's ear, and he tapped it in an effort to clear the fizz.

He and Isabella crouched in a small clearing barely within sight of the cabin. Mike and Cameron had gone in as forward scouts, and sure enough, had found a ring of booby traps encircling the cabin, ranging from old-fashioned loop traps to high-tech pressure pads wired to enough explosives to bring down the mountain.

Worse, the cabin porch was wired to blow. Which had left one important question. How were they going to get in there to rescue the hostages and capture the bounty?

Now, it seemed there was a second question. Where the hell was everyone? The cabin appeared damn near deserted, though all the vehicles were accounted for.

They'd kept watch on the cabin starting the night before, and Mike hadn't seen anyone come or go, but it was becoming rapidly apparent that Boone had another exit. A back door.

"Darn it," Isabella muttered at his side. "We should've moved last night."

Jacob clenched his jaw, knowing she was right, and also suffering with images of what they *had* done the night before, and how it had left him shaken and unsure.

It was supposed to have been a final chance to get it out of their systems once and for all. But damn, if it hadn't felt like something else entirely.

Like a beginning. At least to him.

But since they'd woken up together and brazened the walk of shame out to the vehicles, she'd barely looked at him, hadn't spoken to him. Not even her expression had shown a hint of what had happened between them.

Or whether it had affected her as deeply as it had him.

"Wait." Cameron's transmitted voice broke into the tense silence. "Someone's in there."

Jacob tensed immediately and felt Isabella do the same. He could only imagine the strain she was under, knowing she could already have lost her protectees.

He wanted to reach for her hand, but didn't. There would be time enough later for them to discuss what had happened between them.

Once he figured it out for himself.

Then a figure burst from the cabin and there was no time for thinking at all.

Isabella cried, "Hope!" and broke from their position. She bolted toward the cabin, dodging the traps Mike and Cameron had identified, keeping her feet—barely—on the "safe" corridor the men had marked through the woods.

Jacob was right on her heels, the other bounty hunters close behind him.

He saw a pale, drawn woman stagger out of the cabin, swaying beneath the weight of a toddler on each hip. She must not have heard Isabella's shout, because she fixed her eyes on the vehicles in the parking area and stepped in that direction.

"Hope, stop!" Isabella shouted, legs pistoning as she ran toward the cabin. "The porch is wired!"

The woman froze, comprehension splashing into her eyes. One of the girls started to wail. Hope's mouth opened in horror and she fixed her eyes on the plank flooring that seemed so innocent, but hid enough C-4 to crater the mountain.

"There's a path!" Isabella called as she ran. "Follow the boot prints!"

The blonde lifted a foot to take a step in that direction—

And a bloodied figure reeled out of the door, grabbed her arm and dragged her back inside the cabin.

Jacob sped up and burst into the clearing. "Isabella, wait for me!"

Their plan of a careful infiltration was shot, but he didn't want her going in there without backup.

Isabella didn't hesitate. She leaped up the cabin stairs and plunged through the door.

Jacob heard a shot.

His heart stopped.

A second shot rang out.

And he ran harder.

Isabella!

LYLE'S FIRST BULLET whizzed past Isabella's cheek with a burn of flame and fear. His second shot caught her high on her left arm, spinning her around and punching her into the door frame.

She dived behind a plain-looking sofa in the center of the room, but held her fire. Her arm screamed with pain as her brain took a snapshot of the scene.

Lyle had his arm across Hope's throat and a gun in his off hand. Kane had the girls, one under each arm, where they struggled and screamed, adding noise to the chaos.

Damn it. How had this gone so wrong so quickly?

Not sparing a thought for her injury, though grateful it was in her left arm, not her shooting side, Isabella risked another look, took another mental snapshot as she'd been taught.

She ducked a third shot, but she'd had her look.

Lyle and Kane were backing their hostages toward the rear of the cabin. They could be planning to barricade themselves into a back room.

Or they could be making for the second exit, the one the others must have already used.

Knowing she couldn't let them reach the exit, that it was up to her to protect Hope and the girls, Isabella looked around for help, for backup, for a distraction, for anything.

For Jacob, though she didn't admit to herself she was looking for him until she saw his shadow just outside the door.

He peeked around the door frame and their eyes met. An indefinable current ran between them, communication without words.

You go, I'll cover, his eyes seemed to say.

She nodded slightly and mouthed, *Stay safe.*

You, too. He pressed his lips together and stared at

her a heartbeat longer, as though willing her to understand.

But she didn't. She didn't understand what he wanted to say. She understood her duty, her need to go after the hostages. She understood the job.

And she understood herself better now, understood what had happened the night before—at least for her.

She caught his eyes, held them, and mouthed, *I love you*.

Then she turned, leaped over the couch with gun in hand, and charged in the direction the men had taken the hostages.

JACOB LUNGED in her wake, mind spinning.

I love you.

She'd said it before, back when they'd both been young, and he had cringed at the connection the words implied, the commitment. But now, at the end of their time together, his heart leaped at the words, finally understanding them.

Finally accepting them.

Just as she wasn't her mother, he wasn't either of his parents. He didn't have to be ruled by a relationship, or even a marriage.

It could be a partnership. Isabella and him.

If she survived, he thought, fear clutching his guts. He'd seen the blood on her arm, the hitch in her stride. And now, as he bolted into a dark room behind her, he saw his worst possible nightmare.

Lyle, his bounty, drawing down on Isabella.

The woman he loved.

Jacob charged into the room, shouting. Hope twisted away from Lyle with a surprising burst of strength and kicked at Kane, who still held the squalling babies.

Jacob grabbed the woman's arm, yanked her away and shoved her out into the main room of the cabin. Ignoring her scream, he slammed the door and advanced on the men.

Lyle held Isabella. His arm was across her throat, his eyes crazed, flickering between Jacob and Kane, who growled the toddlers to silence.

Utter silence.

Jacob could hear the men breathing fast, hear his own heart in his ears. He swept his weapon, trying to cover both men, trying to make a choice, should one be necessary.

He could drop Lyle and save Isabella, but it would mean endangering the babies. Or he could drop Kane and trust Isabella to take care of herself.

Her eyes begged him for the second option. She wouldn't thank him for saving her at the expense of her protectees.

Or was there a third option?

Slowly, ever so slowly, Jacob lowered his weapon until he held his hands to his sides. "You can leave them and go."

When Lyle didn't get it right away, Jacob raised his voice. "Go on. Get out of here!"

Isabella caught her breath. Knowledge flashed in her eyes.

Jacob was giving up the bounty.

Jacob, who never, ever, missed what he was aiming at.

Only this time, he was aiming to keep Isabella and the girls safe at all costs. He saw the tension flow out of Lyle, saw the bastard nod slightly at Kane, who loosened his grip and let the toddlers slide to the floor, where they curled into little whimpering balls.

Kane took a step back, toward an open door that led to a set of stairs disappearing down into the earth. Another step.

Jacob's heart clenched at the look in Isabella's eyes, and he said a silent prayer that she'd let it go. That she'd live to fight another day.

Lyle loosened his grip on her.

And all hell broke loose.

Cameron broke through the door at Jacob's back, weapon drawn. Isabella drove her elbow into Lyle's gut and grabbed for the gun.

And missed.

Lyle roared a curse. Kane spun and charged back into the fray.

"Murphy! Get the kids!" Jacob shouted, trusting his boss to get the girls out of the room. The words weren't even out of his mouth before he was diving toward Isabella, who grappled with a cornered, enraged Lyle.

"Bastard!" Kane hit Jacob broadside before he reached the struggling pair. The men fell to the floor in a messy tangle as Cameron scooped up the girls and bolted for the front of the cabin.

Kane punched Jacob on the temple, making his head ring. Jacob grabbed the other man by the hair, reversed their positions and banged Kane's head against the wood floor.

He wasn't in the mood for fighting niceties. He needed to get to Isabella.

Kane dropped back, dazed, and Jacob tore himself away. He staggered to his feet and lurched toward the other struggling pair just in time to see Lyle grab his weapon from the floor—he must have lost it in the struggle—and point it at Isabella's throat.

For once in his life, pure, red rage was Jacob's friend. It rose up, overwhelmed him and sent him hurtling into the fray. He kicked the gun from Lyle's hand, grabbed the bastard by his collar and dragged all one-hundred-eighty pounds or so of him up off the floor.

Off Isabella, who struggled to her feet, grabbed her loose gun and trained it over Jacob's shoulder. "Drop it!"

He heard a third weapon clatter to the floor and knew she'd just saved him from Kane. That made them even.

Or nearly so.

To make them fully even, he drove his fist into Lyle's stomach once, twice and a third time, leaving the piece of garbage gasping for breath. Then he dropped him in a heap and growled, "That was for messing with Isabella in the first place."

AND DAMN if he didn't sound possessive as he said it, Isabella thought. Wondering about it, questioning what—if anything—it might mean, she turned to say something to him—

And a blur erupted from the hidden tunnel and flew toward Lyle's prone body. "You bastard! What have you done to them? I'll kill you with my bare hands. I'll—"

In a flash, Kane grabbed the distraught man—Secretary of Defense Louis Cooper—and clapped a weapon to his head.

Cooper's eyes rolled from his captor to the room at large and fixed on Isabella. His expression darkened with rage. "You! I told you to stay away. I told you to leave us alone! What have you done? Where's my wife and children? Damn you, if you've endangered them, I'll kill you myself!"

He continued shouting, with every word proving for once and all that he was nothing more than a loving husband and father who'd been sucked into events beyond his control. He hadn't set them up. He'd been trying to do as he'd been told.

But all that was secondary now. Her primary purpose, her primary goal was, as it had always been, to protect her man. There was no time for hesitation now, no time for insecurities.

There was only time for the job.

She felt Jacob at her back and took strength from his steadiness. She saw Kane, saw his mouth stretch in a threat, saw his finger tighten on the trigger held beside Louis Cooper's head. She saw all that in a split-second mental snapshot, as she had been trained to do.

And she fired.

As she had been trained to do.

Kane crumpled. His weapon fell to the floor. And Secretary of Defense Cooper looked at her, stunned. His mouth worked. He swallowed hard and said, "Where's Hope?"

"In there." Isabella nodded behind her and gloried in

the rising wail of an overwrought little girl who was now safe, thanks to the bounty hunters.

Thanks to her and Jacob.

Cooper staggered past her, but paused and turned before pushing into the other room. He looked down at her, seeming grayer than he ought in the bright light of day.

"Thank you." He reached out as though to shake her hand, but stopped and simply said, "Thank you."

HOPE SAW LOUIS the moment he stepped through the door. She wasn't surprised to see him come in that way, since Boone and his men had used the entrance almost exclusively. And she wasn't surprised to see how drawn he looked, how haggard.

Always, beside the fear for herself and their daughters, had been her fear for what he was going through.

She wasn't surprised by any of that. But she was surprised to find herself bursting into tears and throwing herself into her husband's arms.

She was home.

ISABELLA SAW the reunion, saw Jacob gesture for Cameron and the others to handcuff Lyle and drag him away, to get Kane's body out of the room. She saw him send Mike and Tony into the tunnel after the other missing men, who she feared were long gone. And she saw him close the doors at each end of the room, creating an illusion of privacy for the two of them.

She saw all that, but she couldn't move, couldn't react. The world was going gray and she couldn't stop it. Her left arm felt stiff and awkward, her face rubbery and slick with sweat.

Oh, hell. She was going to pass out.

She was conscious of familiar arms catching her before she hit the ground, of a familiar voice talking in her ear. She was conscious of motion, the sway of a vehicle, and a hand that never left hers.

A hand that held on tight.

When she came to, she found herself in a narrow hospital bed, and that hand was still hanging on.

"Hey," she said, and felt Jacob's fingers tighten on hers.

"Hey," he said gruffly. "Welcome back."

She took a quick survey. Bandage on right arm. Sore places everywhere. The warm lassitude of good drugs. She turned toward him, noting the tension drawn beside his mouth. She smiled and said, "I guess I'll to live to fight another day."

He winced. "Don't even think about it. No more fighting for you, at least not for a while." He sobered, eyes searching hers for something. "I've got a favor to ask you."

Tingles of nerves ran just below her skin. "What?"

"I want you to stay with me for a while." When she stiffened, he said, "If Cooper didn't set us up, Boone must have tracked you all the way to D.C. and back. Derek Horton and Kane are both dead, and Lyle's back at The Fortress, but Boone and the others are still at large. Until they're captured, you're in danger."

He watched her out of the corner of his eye, as though wondering whether she was going to buy it.

She didn't. Drugs or no drugs, she wasn't letting him off easily. Not this time. Not ever again.

Brain clearing, she struggled up until her spine was pressed against the pillow, her shoulders against the metal headboard. "Try again. Why do you want me to stay with you?"

He scowled. "To keep you safe. If King Aleksandr was behind the abduction—"

"Not good enough," she interrupted. "Now that his family is safe, Cooper will speak to my superiors and get me reinstated at the Service. They can protect me as well as anyone." She narrowed her eyes at him, needing him to say it. "What aren't you telling me?"

He glared at her, frustrated. He rose and paced away, then back, rubbing his hands across his face in his characteristic never-ending motion. Then he stopped, let his hands fall away, and looked down at her with an utterly baffled, utterly vulnerable expression on his face. "I owe you a future claim." He took a breath. "You asked what I wanted and I lied. So I'm not lying now. I want you to stay with me. I want you to give me a chance. I want you to give *us* a chance." He spread his hands as though leaving himself wide open for a bullet. "I want you. Period."

"And?" she demanded, even as her heart thundered in her chest and her soul expanded in a glowing mass that nearly floated her off the bed.

"And," he said, looking down at her with eyes that were finally clear of reservations and confusion, "I love you."

She felt like whooping, like cheering, like doing a

dance around the bed. But instead she grinned fiercely and said, "Then I claim all your futures, Jacob Powell. Just try to get rid of me again."

"Never." He joined her to sit at the edge of the bed, and enfolded her in his arms, at first tentatively, then with more and more pressure, as though he'd wondered, as she had, whether they would ever touch again.

Then he kissed her, or she kissed him, it didn't matter anymore who initiated the moment, it was finally *here*. And as she slid into the kiss, into the future, Isabella thought to herself that this was one game both of them had lost.

And both of them had won.

* * * * *

Don't miss next month's tale of fast-paced
suspense and heart-stopping romance
when BIG SKY BOUNTY HUNTERS *continues*
with WARRIOR SPIRIT *by reader-favorite*
Cassie Miles, only from
Harlequin Intrigue!

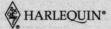

If you enjoyed what you just read,
then we've got an offer you can't resist!

Take 2 bestselling love stories FREE!

Plus get a FREE surprise gift!

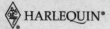

HARLEQUIN®

INTRIGUE

As the summer comes to a close, things really begin to heat up as Harlequin Intrigue presents...

Big Sky Bounty Hunters: No man's a match for these Montana tough guys...but a woman's another story.

Don't miss this brand-new series from some of your favorite authors!

GOING TO EXTREMES
BY AMANDA STEVENS
August 2005

BULLSEYE
BY JESSICA ANDERSEN
September 2005

WARRIOR SPIRIT
BY CASSIE MILES
October 2005

FORBIDDEN CAPTOR
BY JULIE MILLER
November 2005

RILEY'S RETRIBUTION
BY RUTH GLICK,
writing as Rebecca York
December 2005

Available at your favorite retail outlet.